BEFORE H

(A MACKENZIE WHITE

BLAKE PIERCE

ISBN: 978-1-63291-679-2

BOOKS BY BLAKE PIERCE

RILEY PAIGE MYSTERY SERIES
ONCE GONE (Book #1)
ONCE TAKEN (Book #2)
ONCE CRAVED (Book #3)

MACKENZIE WHITE MYSTERY SERIES
BEFORE HE KILLS (Book #1)

PROLOGUE

Any other time, the dawn's first light on the tops of the cornstalks would look beautiful to her. She watched as the first light of day danced along the stalks, creating a muted gold color, and she tried with all she had to find the beauty in it.

She had to distract herself—or else the pain would be unbearable.

She was tied to a large wooden pole that ran up her back and stopped two feet above her head. Her hands were bound behind her, tied together behind the pole. She wore only black lace underwear and a bra that pushed her already generous breasts closer together and higher up. It was the bra that got her the most tips at the strip club, the bra that made her breasts look like they still belonged to a twenty-one-year-old rather than a thirty-four-year-old mother of two.

The pole grated against her bare back, rubbing it raw. But it was not nearly as bad as the pain that the man with the dark, creepy voice had been doling out.

She tensed as she heard him walking behind her, his footsteps falling softly in the clearing of the cornfield. There was another sound, too, fainter. He was dragging something. The whip, she realized, the one he'd been using to beat her. It must have been barbed with something, and had a fanned tail to it. She'd only caught sight of it once—and that had been more than enough.

Her back stung with dozens of lashes, and just hearing the thing being pulled across the ground gave her a rush of panic. She let out a scream—what felt like the hundredth one of the night—that seemed to fall dead and flat in the cornfield. At first, her screams had been cries for help, hoping someone might hear her. But over time, they had become garbled howls of anguish, cries uttered by someone who knew that no one was coming to help her.

"I will consider letting you go," the man said.

He had the voice of someone that either smoked or screamed a lot. There was some sort of odd lisp to his words as well.

"But first, you must confess your crimes."

He'd said this four times. She wracked her brains again, wondering. She had no crimes to confess. She had been a good person to everyone she knew, a good mother—not as good as she would have liked—but she had tried.

What did he want from her?

1

She screamed again and tried bending her back against the pole. When she did, she felt the briefest give to the ropes around her wrists. She also felt her sticky blood pooling around the rope.

"Confess your crimes," he repeated.

"I don't know what you're talking about!" she moaned.

"You will remember," he said.

He'd said that before, too. And he'd said it just before every—

There was a soft whispering noise as the whip arced through the air.

She screamed and writhed against the pole as the thing struck her.

New blood flowed from her new wound but she barely felt it. Instead, she focused on her wrists. The blood that had been collecting there over the last hour or so was mixing with her sweat. She could feel empty space between the rope and her wrists and she thought she might be able to get away. She felt her mind trying to drift away, to disconnect from the situation.

Crack!

This one hit her directly on the shoulder and she bellowed.

"Please," she said. "I'll do anything you want! Just let me go!"

"Confess your—"

She yanked as hard as she could, bringing her arms forward. Her shoulders screamed in agony, but she was instantly free. There was a slight burn as the rope caught the top of her hand, but that was nothing compared to the pain laced across her back.

She yanked forward so hard that she nearly fell to her knees, almost ruining her escape. But the primitive need to survive took control of her muscles and before she was even aware of what she was doing, she was running.

She sprinted, amazed that she was really free, amazed that her legs worked after being bound so long. She would not stop to question it.

She went crashing through the corn, the stalks slapping at her. The leaves and branches seemed to reach out for her, brushing her lacerated back like old withered fingers. She was gasping for breath and focusing on keeping one foot in front of the other. She knew the highway was somewhere nearby. All she had to do was keep running and ignoring the pain.

Behind her, the man started laughing. His voice made the laughter sound like it came from a monster who had been hiding in the cornfield for centuries.

She whimpered and ran on, her bare feet slapping against the dirt and her mostly bare body knocking cornstalks askew. Her breasts bobbed up and down in a ridiculous manner, her left one escaping the bra. She promised herself in that moment that if she made it out of here alive, she would never strip again. She'd find some better job, a better way to provide for her kids.

That lit a new spark in her, and she ran faster, crashing through the corn. She ran as hard as she could. She'd be free of him if she just kept running. The highway had to be right around the corner. Right?

Maybe. But even so, there was no guarantee that anyone would be on it. It wasn't even six AM yet and the Nebraska highways were often very lonesome this time of the day.

Ahead of her, there came a break in the stalks. Dawn's murky light spilled toward her, and her heart leapt to see the highway.

She burst through, and as she did, to her disbelief she heard the noise of an approaching engine. She soared with hope.

She saw the glow of approaching headlights and she ran even faster, so close that she could smell the heat-drenched blacktop.

She reached the edge of the cornfield just as a red pickup truck was passing by. She screamed and waved her arms frantically.

"PLEASE!" she cried.

But to her horror, the truck roared by.

She waved her arms, weeping. Maybe if the driver happened to look into his rearview mirror—

Crack!

A sharp and biting pain exploded along the back of her left knee, and she fell to the ground.

She screamed and tried to get to her feet, but she felt a strong hand grab her by the back of her hair, and soon he was dragging her back into the cornfield.

She tried to move, to break free, but this time, she could not.

There came one last crack of the whip when, finally, gratefully, she lost consciousness.

Soon, she knew, it would all come to an end: the noise, the whip, the pain—and her brief, pain-filled life.

3

CHAPTER ONE

Detective Mackenzie White braced herself for the worst as she walked through the cornfield that afternoon. The sound of the cornstalks unnerved her as she passed through them, a dead sound, grazing her jacket as she passed through row after row. The clearing she sought, it seemed, was miles away.

She finally reached it, and as she did, she stopped cold, wishing she were anywhere but here. There was a dead, mostly naked body of a thirty-something female tied to a pole, her face frozen in an expression of anguish. It was an expression that Mackenzie wished she'd never seen—and knew she would never forget.

Five policemen milled around the clearing, doing nothing in particular. They were trying to look busy but she knew they were simply trying to make sense of it. She felt certain that none of them had seen anything like this before. It took no more than five seconds of seeing the blonde woman tied to the wooden pole before Mackenzie knew there was something much deeper going on here. Something unlike anything she had ever encountered. This was not what happened in the cornfields of Nebraska.

Mackenzie approached the body and walked a slow circle around it. As she did, she sensed the other officers watching her. She knew that some of them felt she took her job far too seriously. She approached things a little too closely, looked for threads and connections that were almost abstract in nature. She was the young woman who had reached the position of detective far too fast in the eyes of a lot of the men at the precinct, she knew. She was the ambitious girl that everyone assumed had her eyes on bigger and better things than a detective with small-town Nebraska law enforcement.

Mackenzie ignored them. She focused solely on the body, waving away the flies that darted everywhere. They hovered spastically around the woman's body, creating a small black cloud, and the heat was doing the body no favors. It had been hot all summer and it felt as if all of that heat had been collected in this cornfield and placed here.

Mackenzie came close and studied her, trying to repress a feeling of nausea and a wave of sadness. The woman's back was covered in gashes. They looked uniform in nature, likely placed there by the same instrument. Her back was covered in blood, mostly dried and sticky. The back of her thong underwear was caked in it, too.

As Mackenzie finished her loop around the body, a short but stout policeman approached her. She knew him well, though she didn't care for him.

"Hello, Detective White," Chief Nelson said.

"Chief," she replied.

"Where's Porter?"

There was nothing condescending in his voice, but she felt it nonetheless. This hardened local fifty-something police chief did not want a twenty-five-year-old woman helping to make sense of this case. Walter Porter, her fifty-five-year-old partner, would be best for the job.

"Back at the highway," Mackenzie said. "He's speaking to the farmer that discovered the body. He'll be along shortly."

"Okay," Nelson said, clearly a little more at ease. "What do you make of this?"

Mackenzie wasn't sure how to answer that. She knew he was testing her. He did it from time to time, even on menial things at the precinct. He didn't do it to any of the other officers or detectives, and she was fairly certain he only did it to her because she was young and a woman.

Her gut told her this was more than some theatrical murder. Was it the countless lashes on her back? Was it the fact that the woman had a body that was pin-up worthy? Her breasts were clearly fake and if Mackenzie had to guess, her rear had seen some work as well. She was wearing a good deal of makeup, some of which had been smeared and smudged from tears.

"I think," Mackenzie said, finally answering Nelson's question, "that this was purely a violent crime. I think forensics will show no sexual abuse. Most men that kidnap a woman for sex rarely abuse their victim this much, even if they plan to kill them later. I also think the style of underwear she is wearing suggests that she was a woman of provocative nature. Quite honestly, judging by her makeup style and the ample size of her breasts, I'd start placing calls to strip clubs in Omaha to see if any dancers were MIA last night."

"All of that has already been done," Nelson replied smugly. "The deceased is Hailey Lizbrook, thirty-four years old, a mother of two boys and a mid-level dancer at The Runway in Omaha."

He recited these facts as if he were reading an instruction manual. Mackenzie assumed he'd been in his position long enough where murder victims were no longer people, but simply a puzzle to be solved.

But Mackenzie, only a few years into her career, was not so hardened and heartless. She studied the woman with an eye toward figuring out what had happened, but also saw her as a woman who had left two boys behind—boys that would live the rest of their lives without a mother. For a mother of two to be a stripper, Mackenzie assumed that there were money troubles in her life and that she was willing to do damn near anything to provide for her kids. But now here she was, strapped to a pole and partially mauled by some faceless man that—

The rustling of cornstalks from behind her cut her off. She turned to see Walter Porter coming through the corn. He looked annoyed as he entered the clearing, wiping dirt and corn silk from his coat.

He looked around for a moment before his eyes settled on Hailey Lizbrook's body on the pole. A surprised smirk came across his face, his grayed moustache tilting to the right at a harsh angle. He then looked to Mackenzie and Nelson and wasted no time coming over.

"Porter," Chief Nelson said. "White's solving this thing already. She's pretty sharp."

"She can be," Porter said dismissively.

It was always like this. Nelson wasn't genuinely paying her a compliment. He was, in fact, teasing Porter for being stuck with the pretty young girl who had come out of nowhere and yanked up the position of detective—the pretty young girl that few men in the precinct over the age of thirty took seriously. And God, did Porter hate it.

While she *did* enjoy watching Porter writhe under the teasing, it wasn't worth feeling inadequate and underappreciated. Time and again she had solved cases the other men couldn't and this, she knew, threatened them. She was only twenty-five, far too young to start feeling burnt out in a career that she once loved. But now, being stuck with Porter, and with this force, she was starting to hate it.

Porter made an effort to step between Nelson and Mackenzie, letting her know that this was his show now. Mackenzie felt herself starting to fume, but she choked it down. She'd been choking it down for the last three months, ever since she'd been assigned to work with him. From day one, Porter had made no secret about his dislike for her. After all, she had replaced Porter's partner of twenty-eight years who had been released from the force, as far as Porter was concerned, to make room for a young female.

6

Mackenzie ignored his blatant disrespect; she refused to let it affect her work ethic. Without a word, she went back to the body. She studied it closely. It hurt to study it, and yet, as far as she was concerned, there was no dead body that would ever affect her as much as the first she had ever seen. She was almost reaching the point where she no longer saw her father's body when she stepped onto a murder scene. But not yet. She'd been seven years old when she walked into the bedroom and saw him half-sprawled on the bed, in a pool of blood. And she had never stopped seeing it since.

Mackenzie searched for clues that this murder had not been about sex. She saw no signs of bruising or scratching on her breasts or buttocks, no external bleeding around the vagina. She then looked to the woman's hands and feet, wondering if there might be a religious motive; signs of puncture along the palms, ankles, and feet could denote a reference to crucifixion. But there were no signs of that, either.

In the brief report she and Porter had been given, she knew the victim's clothes had not been located. Mackenzie thought this likely meant that the killer had them, or had disposed of them. This indicated to her that he was either cautious, or borderline obsessive. Add that to the fact that his motives last night had almost certainly not been of a sexual nature, and it added up to a potentially elusive and calculated killer.

Mackenzie backed to the edge of the clearing and took in the entirety of the scene. Porter gave her a sideways glance and then ignored her completely, continuing to talk to Nelson. She noticed that the other policemen were watching her. Some of them, at least, were watching her work. She'd come into the role of detective with a reputation for being exceptionally bright and highly regarded by the majority of instructors at the police academy, and from time to time, younger cops—men and women alike—would ask her genuine questions or seek her opinion.

On the other hand, she knew that a few of the men sharing the clearing with her might also be leering, too. She wasn't sure which was worse: the men that checked out her ass when she walked by or the ones that laughed behind her back at the little girl trying to play the role of bad-ass detective.

As she studied the scene, she was once again assaulted by the nagging suspicion that something was terribly wrong here. She felt like she was opening up a book, reading page one of a story that she knew had some very difficult pages ahead.

This is just the beginning, she thought.

She looked to the dirt around the pole and saw a few scuffed boot marks, but not anything that would provide prints. There was also a series of shapes in the dirt that looked almost serpentine. She squatted down for a closer look and saw that several of the shapes trailed side by side, winding their way around the wooden pole in a broken fashion, as if whatever made them had circled the pole several times. She then looked to the woman's back and saw that the gashes in her flesh were roughly the same shape of the markings on the ground.

"Porter," she said.

"What is it?" he asked, clearly annoyed that he'd been interrupted.

"I think I've got weapon prints here."

Porter hesitated for a second and then walked over to where Mackenzie was hunkered down in the dirt. When he squatted down next to her, he groaned slightly and she could hear his belt creaking. He was about fifty pounds overweight and it was showing more and more as he closed in on fifty-five.

"A whip of some kind?" he asked.

"Looks like it."

She examined the ground, following the marks in the sand all the way up to the pole—and while doing so, she noticed something else. It was something minuscule, so small that she almost didn't catch it.

She walked over to the pole, careful not to touch the body before forensics could get to it. She again hunkered down and when she did, she felt the full weight of the afternoon's heat pressing down on her. Undaunted, she craned her head closer to the pole, so close that her forehead nearly touched it.

"What the hell are you doing?" Nelson asked.

"Something's carved here," she said. "Looks like numbers."

Porter came over to investigate but did everything he could not to bend down again. "White, that chunk of wood is easily twenty years old," he said. "That carving looks just as old."

"Maybe," Mackenzie said. But she didn't think so.

Already uninterested in the discovery, Porter went back to speaking with Nelson, comparing notes about information he'd gotten from the farmer who had discovered the body.

Mackenzie took out her phone and snapped a picture of the numbers. She enlarged the image and the numbers became a bit clearer. Seeing them in such detail once again made her feel as if this was all the start of something much bigger.

The numbers meant nothing to her. Maybe Porter was right; maybe they meant absolutely nothing. Maybe they'd been carved there by a logger when the post had been created. Maybe some bored kid had chiseled them there somewhere along the years.

But that didn't feel right.

Nothing about this felt right.

And she knew, in her heart, that this was only the beginning.

CHAPTER TWO

Mackenzie felt a knot in her stomach as she looked out of the car and saw the news vans piled up, reporters jockeying for the best position to assault her and Porter as they pulled up to the precinct. As Porter parked, she watched several news anchors approach, running across the precinct lawn with burdened cameramen keeping pace behind them.

Mackenzie saw Nelson already at the front doors, doing what he could to pacify them, looking uncomfortable and agitated. Even from here she could see the sweat glistening on his forehead.

As they got out, Porter ambled up beside her, making sure she was not the first detective the media saw. As he passed her, he said, "Don't you tell these vampires anything."

She felt a rush of indignation at his condescending comment.

"I know, Porter."

The throng of reporters and cameras reached them. There were at least a dozen mics sticking out of the crowd and into their faces as they made their way past. The questions came at them like the buzzing of insects.

"Have the victim's children been notified yet?"

"What was the farmer's reaction when he found the body?"

"Is this a case of sexual abuse?"

"Is it wise for a woman to be assigned to such a case?"

That last one stung Mackenzie a bit. Sure, she knew they were simply trying to land a response, hoping for a juicy twenty-second spot for the afternoon newscast. It was only four o'clock; if they acted quickly, they might have a nugget for the six o'clock news.

As she made her way through the doors and inside, that last question echoed like thunder in her head.

Is it wise for a woman to be assigned to such a case?

She recalled how emotionlessly Nelson had read off Hailey Lizbrook's information.

Of course it is, Mackenzie thought. *In fact, it's crucial.*

Finally they entered the precinct and the doors slammed behind them. Mackenzie breathed with relief to be in the quiet.

"Fucking leeches," Porter said.

He'd dropped the swagger from his step now that he was no longer in front of the cameras. He walked slowly past the receptionist's desk and toward the hallway that led to the conference rooms and offices that made up their precinct. He

10

looked tired, ready to go home, ready to be done with this case already.

Mackenzie entered the conference room first. There were several officers sitting at a large table, some in uniform and some in their street clothes. Given their presence and the sudden appearance of the news vans, Mackenzie guessed that the story had leaked in all sorts of directions in the two and a half hours between leaving her office, heading to the cornfield, and getting back. It was more than a random grisly murder; now, it had become a spectacle.

Mackenzie grabbed a cup of coffee and took a seat at the table. Someone had already set folders around the table with the little bit of information that had already been gathered about the case. As she looked through it, more people started filing into the room. Porter eventually entered, taking a seat at the opposite end.

Mackenzie took a moment to check her phone and found that she had eight missed calls, five voice messages, and a dozen e-mails. It was a stark reminder that she'd already had a full caseload before being sent out to the cornfield this morning. The sad irony was that while her older peers spent a lot of time demeaning her and throwing subtle insults her way, they also realized her talents. As a result, she kept one of the larger caseloads on the force. To date, though, she had never fallen behind and had a stellar rate of closed cases.

She thought about answering some of the e-mails while she waited, but Chief Nelson came in before she could get the chance. He quickly closed the conference room door behind him.

"I don't know how the media found out about this so quickly," he growled, "but if I find out that someone in this room is responsible, there's going to be hell to pay."

The room fell quiet. A few officers and related staff started to look nervously at the contents of the folders in front of them. While Mackenzie didn't care much for Nelson, there was no denying that the man's presence and voice commanded a room without much effort.

"Here's where we stand," Nelson said. "The victim is Hailey Lizbrook, a stripper from Omaha. Thirty-four years old, two boys, ages nine and fifteen. From what we can gather, she was abducted before clocking in for work, as her employer says she never showed up the night before. Security footage from the Runway, her place of employment, shows nothing. So we're working on the assumption that she was taken somewhere between her apartment and the Runway. That's an area of seven and a half miles—an area that we currently have a few bodies investigating with the Omaha PD right now."

He then looked to Porter as if he were a prized pupil and said:

"Porter, why don't you describe the scene?"

Of course he'd choose Porter.

Porter stood up and looked around the room as if to make sure everyone was paying close attention.

"The victim was bound to a wooden pole with her hands tied behind her. The sight of her death was in a clearing in a cornfield, a little less than a mile off the highway. Her back was covered in what appeared to be lash marks, placed there by some sort of a whip. We noted prints in the dirt that were the same shape and size of the lashes. While we won't know for absolutely certain until after the coroner's report, we are fairly certain this was not a sexual attack, even though the victim had been stripped to her underwear and her clothes were nowhere to be found."

"Thanks, Porter," Nelson said. "Speaking of the coroner, I spoke with him on the phone about twenty minutes ago. He says that while he won't know for sure until an autopsy is conducted, the cause of death is likely going to be blood loss or some sort trauma—likely to the head or heart."

His eyes then went to Mackenzie and there was very little interest in them when he asked: "Anything to add, White?"

"The numbers," she said.

Nelson rolled his eyes in front of the entire room. It was a clear sign of disrespect but she trudged past it, determined to get it out to everyone present before she could be cut off.

"I discovered what appeared to be two numbers, separated by a slash, carved into the bottom of the pole."

"What were the numbers?" one of the younger officers at the table asked.

"Numbers and letters actually," Mackenzie said. "N 511 and J 202. I have a picture on my phone."

"Other pictures will be here shortly, just as soon as Nancy gets them printed out," Nelson said. He spoke quickly and forcefully, letting the room know that the issue of these numbers was now closed.

Mackenzie listened to Nelson as he droned on about the tasks that needed to be carried out to cover the seven-and-a-half-mile area between Hailey Lizbrook's home and the Runway. But she was only half-listening, really. Her mind kept going back to the way the woman's body had been strung up. Something about the entire display of the body had seemed almost familiar to her right away, and it still stuck with her as she sat in the conference room.

She went through the brief notes in the folder, hoping some small detail might trigger something in her memory. She leafed through the four pages of information, hoping to uncover something. She already knew everything in the folder, but she scanned the details anyway.

Thirty-four-year-old female, presumed killed the previous night. Lashes, cuts, various abrasions on her back, tied to an old wooden post. Cause of death assumed to be blood loss or possible trauma to the heart. Method of binding suggests possible religious overtones while woman's body type hints at sexual motivations.

As she read through it, something clicked. She zoned out a bit, allowing her mind to go where it needed without interference from her surroundings.

As she put the dots together, coming up with a connection she *hoped* she was wrong about, Nelson started to wind down.

"…and since it's too late for roadblocks to be effective, we're going to have to rely mostly on witness testimony, even down to the most minute and seemingly useless detail. Now, does anyone have anything else to add?"

"One thing, sir," Mackenzie said.

She could tell that Nelson was containing a sigh. From the other end of the table, she heard Porter make a soft sort of chuckling noise. She ignored it all and waited to see how Nelson would address her.

"Yes, White?" he asked.

"I'm recalling a case in 1987 that was similar to this. I'm pretty sure it was right outside of Roseland. The binding was the same, the type of woman was the same. I'm fairly certain the method of beating was the same."

"1987?" Nelson asked. "White, were you even born yet?"

This was met with soft laughter from more than half of the room. Mackenzie let it slide right off. She'd find the time to be embarrassed later.

"I was not," she said, not afraid to tangle with him. "But I *did* read the report."

"You forget, sir," Porter said. "Mackenzie spends her free time reading cold case files. The girl is like a walking encyclopedia for this stuff."

Mackenzie noticed at once that Porter had referred to her by her first name *and* called her a girl rather than a woman. The sad thing was that she didn't think he was even aware of the disrespect.

13

Nelson rubbed at his head and finally let out the thunderous sigh that had been building up. "1987? You're sure?"

"Almost positive."

"Roseland?"

"Or the immediate surrounding area," she said.

"Okay," Nelson said, looking to the far end of the table where a middle-aged woman sat, listening diligently. There was a laptop in front of her, which she had been quietly typing on the whole time. "Nancy, can you run a search for that in the database?"

"Yes sir," she said. She started typing something into the precinct's internal server right away.

Nelson cast Mackenzie another disapproving look that essentially translated to: *You better be right. If not, you just wasted twenty seconds of my valuable time.*

"All right, boys and ladies," Nelson said. "Here's how we're going to break this out. The moment this meeting ends, I want Smith and Berryhill heading out to Omaha to help the local PD out there. From there, if needed, we'll rotate out in pairs. Porter and White, want you two to speak with the kids of the deceased and her employer. We're also working on getting the address of her sister."

"Excuse me, sir," Nancy said, looking up from her computer.

"Yes, Nancy?"

"It seems Detective White was right. October of 1987, a prostitute was found dead and bound to a wooden line pole just outside of the Roseland city limits. The file I'm looking at says she was stripped to her underwear and flogged severely. No signs of sexual abuse and no motive to speak of."

The room went quiet again as many damning questions went unspoken. Finally, it was Porter that spoke up and although Mackenzie could tell he was trying to dismiss the case, she could hear a hint of worry in his voice.

"That's almost thirty years ago," he said. "I'd call that a flimsy connection."

"But it's a connection nonetheless," Mackenzie said.

Nelson slammed a hefty hand down on the desk, his eyes burning into Mackenzie. "If there *is* a connection here, you know what it means, right?"

"It means we may be dealing with a serial killer," she said. "And even the *idea* that we may be dealing with a serial killer means we need to consider calling in the FBI."

"Ah, hell," Nelson said. "You're jumping the gun there. You're jumping an entire arsenal, in fact."

"With all due respect," Mackenzie said, "it's worth looking into."

"And now that your hardwired brain has brought it to our attention, we *have* to," Nelson said. "I'll make some calls and get you involved in checking it out. For now, let's get cracking on things that are relevant and timely. That's it for now, everyone. Now get to work."

The small group at the conference table started to disperse, taking their folders with them. As Mackenzie started out of the room, Nancy gave her a small smile of acknowledgment. It was the most encouragement Mackenzie had gotten at work in more than two weeks. Nancy was the receptionist and sometimes fact-checker around the precinct. As far as Mackenzie knew, she was one of the few older members on the force who had no real problem with her.

"Porter and White, hold on," Nelson said.

She saw that Nelson was now showing some of the same worry she had seen and heard in Porter when he spoke up moments ago. He looked almost sick with it.

"Good recall on that 1987 case," Nelson told Mackenzie. It looked like it physically hurt him to pay her the compliment. "It *is* a shot in the dark. But it does make you wonder…"

"Wonder what?" Porter asked.

Mackenzie, never one for beating around the bush, answered for Nelson.

"Why he's decided to go active now," she said.

Then she added:

"And when he'll kill again."

CHAPTER THREE

He sat in his car, enjoying the silence. Streetlights cast a ghostly glow on the street. There weren't many cars out at such a late hour, making it eerily tranquil. He knew that anyone out in this part of town at such an hour was likely preoccupied or doing their dealings in secret. It made it easier for him to focus on the work at hand—the Good Work.

The sidewalks were dark except for the occasional neon glow of seedy establishments. The crude figure of a well-endowed woman glowed in the window of the building he was studying. It flickered like a beacon on a stormy sea. But there was no refuge in those places—no respectable refuge, anyway.

As he sat in his car, as far away from the streetlights as he could get, he thought about his collection at home. He'd studied it closely before heading out tonight. There were remnants of his work on his small desk: a purse, an earring, a gold necklace, a chunk of blonde hair placed in a small Tupperware container. They were reminders, reminders that he had been assigned this work. And that he had more work to do.

A man emerged from the building on the opposite side of the street, breaking him from his thoughts. Watching, he sat there and waited patiently. He'd learned a great deal about patience over the years. Because of that, knowing that he must now work quickly made him anxious. What if he was not precise?

He had little choice. Already, Hailey Lizbrook's murder was on the news. People were searching for him—as if he were the one who had done something bad. They just didn't understand. What he had given that woman had been a gift.

An act of grace.

In the past, he'd let much time pass between his sacred acts. But now, an urgency was upon him. There was so much to do. There were always women out there—on street corners, in personal ads, on television.

In the end, they'd understand. They'd understand and they'd thank him. They would ask him how to be pure, and he would open their eyes.

Moments later, the neon image of the woman in the window went black. The glow behind the windows died out. The place had gone dark, the lights cut off as they closed for the night.

He knew this meant that the women would be coming out of the back at any moment, headed to their cars and then home.

He shifted into drive and drove slowly around the block. The streetlights seemed to chase him, but he knew that there were no prying eyes to see him. In this part of the city, no one cared.

At the back of the building, most of the cars were nice. There was good money in keeping your body on display. He parked at the far edge of the lot and waited some more.

After a long while, the employee door finally opened. Two women came out, accompanied by a man that looked like he worked security for the place. He eyed the security man, wondering if he might be a problem. He had a gun under the seat that he would use if he absolutely had to, but he'd rather not. He hadn't had to use it yet. He actually abhorred guns. There was something impure about then, something almost slothful.

Finally, they all split up, getting in their cars and heading off.

He watched others emerge, and then he sat upright. He could feel his heart pounding. That was her. That was the one.

She was short, with fake blonde hair that bobbed just over her shoulders. He watched her get into her car and he did not drive forward until her taillights were around the corner.

He drove around the other side of the building, so as not to draw attention to himself. He trailed behind her, his heart starting to race. Instinctively, he reached under his seat and felt the strand of rope. It eased his nerves.

It calmed him to know that, after the pursuit, there would come the sacrifice.

And come, it would.

CHAPTER FOUR

Mackenzie sat in the passenger seat, several files scattered in her lap, Porter behind the wheel, tapping his fingers to the beat of a Rolling Stones song. He kept the car tuned to the same classic rock station he always listened to while driving, and Mackenzie glanced up, annoyed, her concentration finally broken. She watched the car's headlights slice down the highway at eighty miles per hour, and turned to him.

"Can you please turn that down?" she snapped.

Usually, she didn't mind, but she was trying to slip into the right frame of mind, to understand the killer's MO.

With a sigh and shake of his head, Porter turned down the radio. He glanced over to her dismissively.

"What are you hoping to find, anyway?" he asked.

"I'm not trying to *find* anything," Mackenzie said. "I'm trying to put the pieces together to better understand the killer's personality type. If we can think like him, we have a much better chance of finding him."

"Or," Porter said, "you can just wait until we get to Omaha and speak to the victim's kids and sister like Nelson told us."

Without even looking at him, Mackenzie could tell that he was struggling to keep some wise-ass comment in. She had to give him a little credit, she supposed. When it was just the two of them on the road or at a crime scene, Porter kept the wisecracks and degrading behavior to a minimum.

She ignored Porter for the moment and looked to the notes in her lap. She was comparing the notes from the 1987 case and the Hailey Lizbrook murder. The more she read over them, the more she was convinced that they had been pulled off by the same guy. But the thing that kept frustrating her was that there was no clear motive.

She looked back and forth through the documents, flipping through pages and cycling through the information. She started to murmur to herself, asking questions and stating facts out loud. It was something she had done ever since high school, a quirk that she had never quite grown out of.

"No evidence of sexual abuse in either case," she said softly. "No obvious ties between the victims other than profession. No real chance of religious motivations. Why not go for the full-on crucifix rather than just basic poles if you're going for a religious theme?

The numbers were present in both cases but the numbers don't show any clear significance to the killings."

"Don't take this the wrong way," Porter said, "but I'd really rather be listening to the Stones."

Mackenzie stopped talking to herself and then noticed that her notification light was blinking on her phone. After she and Porter had left, she'd e-mailed Nancy and asked her to do a few quick searches with the terms *pole, stripper, prostitute, waitress, corn, lashes,* and the sequence of numbers *N511/J202* from murder cases over the last thirty years. When Mackenzie checked her phone, she saw that Nancy, as usual, had acted quickly.

The mail Nancy had sent back read: *Not much, I'm afraid. I've attached the briefs on the few cases I did find, though. Good luck!*

There were only five attachments and Mackenzie was able to look through them pretty quickly. Three of them clearly had nothing to do with the Lizbrook murder or the case from '87. But the other two were interesting enough to at least consider.

One of them was a case from 1994 where a woman had been found dead behind an abandoned barn in a rural area about eighty miles outside of Omaha. She had been tied to a wooden pole and it was believed that her body had been there for at least six days before being discovered. Her body had gone stiff and a few woodland animals—believed to be bobcats—had started eating at her legs. The woman had a lengthy criminal record, including two arrests for soliciting sex. Again, there had been no clear signs of sexual abuse and while there had been lashes on her back, they had not been nearly as extensive as what they had found on Hailey Lizbrook. The briefing on the murder said nothing about numbers being found on the pole, though.

The second maybe-related file concerned a nineteen-year-old girl that had been reported as kidnapped when she did not return home for Christmas break from her freshman year at the University of Nebraska in 2009. When her body was discovered in an empty field three months later, partially buried, there had been lashes on her back. Images were later leaked to the press, showing the young girl nude and engaged in some sort of lurid sex party at a fraternity house. The pictures had been taken one week before she had been reported missing.

The last case was a bit of a stretch, but Mackenzie thought they could both potentially be linked to the '87 murder and Hailey Lizbrook.

"What you got there?" Porter asked.

"Nancy sent me briefs from some other cases that might be linked."

"Anything good?"

She hesitated but then filled him in on the two potential links. When she was done, Porter nodded his head as he stared out into the night. They passed a sign telling them that Omaha was twenty-two miles ahead.

"I think you try too hard sometimes," Porter said. "You bust your ass and a lot of people have taken notice. But let's be honest: no matter how hard you try, not every case has some huge link that is going to create some monster case for you."

"So humor me," Mackenzie said. "At this very moment, what does your gut tell you about this case? What are we dealing with?"

"It's just some basic perp with mommy issues," Porter said dismissively. "We talk to enough people, we find him. All this analysis is a waste of time. You don't find people by getting into their head. You find them by asking questions. Street work. Door to door. Witness to witness."

As they fell into silence, Mackenzie started to worry about just how simplistic his view of the world was, how black and white. It left no room for nuance, for anything outside of his predetermined beliefs. She thought the psycho they were dealing with was far too sophisticated for that.

"What's *your* take on our killer?" he finally asked.

She could detect resentment in his voice, as if he really hadn't wanted to ask her but the silence had got the best of him.

"I think he hates women for what they represent," she said softly, working it out in her mind as she spoke. "Maybe he's a fifty-year-old virgin who thinks sex is gross—and yet there's also that *need* in him for sex. Killing women makes him feel like he's conquering his own instincts, instincts he sees as gross and inhuman. If he can eliminate the source of where those sexual urges come from, he feels in control. The lashes on the back indicate that he's almost punishing them, probably for their provocative nature. Then there's the fact that there are no signs of sexual abuse. It makes me wonder if this is some sort of attempt at purity in the killer's eyes."

Porter shook his head, almost like some disappointed parent.

"That's what I'm talking about," he said. "A waste of time. You've got yourself so far into this you don't even know what you think anymore—and none of that is gonna help us. You can't see the forest for the trees."

The awkward silence blanketed them again. Apparently done speaking, Porter turned the radio up.

It lasted only a few minutes, though. As they neared Omaha, Porter turned the radio back down without being prompted this time. Porter spoke up and when he did, he sounded nervous, but Mackenzie could also hear the effort he was putting forth to sound like he was the one in charge.

"You ever interviewed kids after they lost a parent?" Porter asked.

"Once," she said. "After a drive-by. An eleven-year-old boy."

"I've had a few, too. It's not fun."

"No, it's not," Mackenzie agreed.

"Well look, we're about to ask two boys questions about their dead mom. The topic of where she works is bound to come up. We have to handle this thing with kid gloves—no pun intended."

She fumed. He was doing that thing where he spoke down to her as if she were a child.

"Let me lead. You can be the comforting shoulder if they start crying. Nelson says the sister will also be there, but I can't imagine she'd be any reliable source of comfort. She's probably just as wrecked as the kids."

Mackenzie actually didn't think it was the best idea. But she also knew that when Porter and Nelson were involved, she needed to choose her battles wisely. So if Porter wanted to take charge of asking two grieving kids about their dead mom, she'd let him have that weird ego trip.

"As you want," she said through clenched teeth.

The car fell into silence again. This time, Porter kept the radio turned down, the only sounds coming from the shifting of pages in Mackenzie's lap. There was a larger story in those pages and the documents Nancy had sent; Mackenzie was sure of it.

Of course, for the story to be told, all of the characters needed to be revealed. And for now, the central character was still hiding in the shadows.

The car slowed and Mackenzie raised her head as they turned down a quiet block. She felt a familiar pit in her stomach, and she wished she were anywhere but here.

They were about to talk to a dead woman's kids.

CHAPTER FIVE

Mackenzie was surprised as she entered Hailey Lizbrook's apartment; it was not what she had expected. It was neat and tidy, the furniture nicely centered and dusted. The décor was very much that of a domesticated woman, right down to the coffee mugs with cute sayings and the pot holders hanging from ornate hooks by the stove. It was evident that she had run a tight ship, right down to the haircuts and pajamas on her sons.

It was very much like the family and home she always dreamed of having herself.

Mackenzie recalled from the files that the boys were nine and fifteen; the oldest was Kevin and the youngest was Dalton. It was clear as she met him that Dalton had been crying a lot, his blue eyes rimmed with puffy red splotches.

Kevin, on the other hand, looked angry more than anything else. As they settled in and Porter took the lead, it showed perfectly clear when Porter tried speaking to them in a tone that was somewhere between condescending and a preschool teacher trying too hard. Mackenzie winced inside as Porter spoke.

"Now I need to know if your mother had any men friends," Porter said.

He stood in the center of the room while the boys sat on the living room couch. Hailey's sister, Jennifer, was standing in the adjoining kitchen, smoking a cigarette by the stove with the exhaust fan running.

"You mean like a boyfriend?" Dalton asked.

"Sure, that could be a male friend," Porter said. "But I don't even mean like that. Any man that she might have spoken to more than once. Even someone like a mailman or someone at the grocery store."

Both of the boys were looking at Porter as if they were expecting him to perform a magic trick or maybe even spontaneously combust. Mackenzie was doing the same. She had never heard him use such a soft tone. It was almost funny to hear such a soothing tone come out of his mouth.

"No, I don't think so," Dalton said.

"No," Kevin agreed. "And she didn't have a boyfriend, either. Not that I know of."

Mackenzie and Porter looked to Jennifer over by the stove for an answer. All they got in response was a shrug. Mackenzie was pretty sure Jennifer was in some sort of shock. It made her wonder if there might be another family member that could take care of these boys for a while, since Jennifer certainly didn't seem like a fit guardian at the moment.

"Well, how about people that you and your mom didn't get along with?" Porter asked. "Did you ever hear her arguing with anyone?"

Dalton only shook his head. Mackenzie was pretty sure the kid was on the brink of tears again. As for Kevin, he rolled his eyes while looking directly at Porter.

"No," he said. "We're not stupid. We know what you're trying to ask us. You want to know if we can think of anyone that might have killed our mom. Right?"

Porter looked as if he had been punched in the gut. He glanced nervously over to Mackenzie but managed to get his composure back fairly quickly.

"Well, yes," he said. "That's what I'm getting at. But it seems clear that you don't have any information."

"You think?" Kevin said.

There was a tense moment where Mackenzie was certain that Porter was going to get harsh with the kid. Kevin was looking at Porter with pain in his expression, almost daring Porter to keep at him.

"Well," Porter said, "I think I've bothered you boys enough. Thanks for your time."

"Hold on," Mackenzie said, the objection coming out of her mouth before she was able to think about stopping it.

Porter gave her a look that could have melted wax. It was clear that he felt they were wasting their time talking to these two grief-stricken sons—especially a fifteen-year-old that clearly had issues with authority. Mackenzie shrugged his expression off and knelt down to Dalton's eye level.

"Listen, do you think you could go hang out in the kitchen with your aunt for a second?"

"Yeah," Dalton said, his voice ragged and soft.

"Detective Porter, why don't you go with him?"

Again, Porter's gaze toward her was filled with hate. Mackenzie stared right back at him, unflinching. She set her face until it felt like stone and was determined to stand her ground on this one. If he wanted to argue, she'd take it outside. But it was clear that even in a situation with two kids and a nearly catatonic woman, he didn't want to be embarrassed.

"Of course," he finally said through gritted teeth.

Mackenzie waited a moment as Porter and Dalton walked into the kitchen.

Mackenzie stood back up. She knew that around the age of twelve or so, the tactic of getting down at eye level with kids stopped working.

She looked at Kevin and saw that the defiance he had showed Porter was still there. Mackenzie had nothing against teenagers, but she did know that they were often difficult to work with—especially in the midst of tragic circumstances. But she'd seen how Kevin had responded to Porter and thought she might know how to get through to him.

"Level with me, Kevin," she said. "Do you feel like we showed up too soon? Do you think we're being inconsiderate by asking questions so soon after you received the news about your mom?"

"Sort of," he said.

"Do you just not feel like talking right now?"

"No, I'm fine with talking," Kevin said. "But that guy is a dick."

Mackenzie knew this was her chance. She could take a professional, formal approach, as she normally would—or she could use this opportunity to establish a rapport with an angry teenage boy. Teenagers, she knew, above all, cherished honesty. They could see through anything when driven by emotion.

"You're right," she said. "He is a dick."

Kevin stared back at her, wide-eyed. She had stunned him; clearly, he had not expected that response.

"But that doesn't change the fact that I have to work with him," she added, her voice layered with sympathy and understanding. "It also doesn't change the fact that we're here to help you. We want to find whoever did this to your mother. Don't you?"

He was silent for a long time; then, finally, he nodded back.

"Do you think you could talk to me, then?" Mackenzie asked. "Just a few quick questions and then we'll get out of here."

"And who comes after that?" Kevin asked, guarded.

"Honestly?"

Kevin nodded and she saw that he was close to tears. She wondered if he'd been holding them back this entire time, trying to be strong for his brother and his aunt.

"Well, after we leave, we'll call in any information we can get and then social services will come to make sure your aunt Jennifer is suitable to care for you while final arrangements are made for your mom."

"She's cool most of the time," Kevin said, looking over to Jennifer. "But her and Mom were really tight. Like best friends."

"Sisters can be like that," Mackenzie said, having no idea if it was true or not. "But for now, I need to see if you can focus on my questions. Can you do that?"

"Yeah."

"Good. Now, I hate to ask you this, but it's sort of necessary. Do you know what your mom did for work?"

Kevin nodded as his eyes dropped to the floor.

"Yeah," he said. "And I don't know how, but kids at school know about it, too. Someone's horny dad probably went to the club and saw her and recognized her from a school function or something. It sucks. I got ribbed about it all the time."

Mackenzie couldn't imagine that kind of torment but it also made her respect Hailey Lizbrook a hell of a lot more. Sure, she stripped for money at night but during the day she was apparently a mother who was involved with her kids.

"Okay," Mackenzie said. "So, knowing about her job, you can imagine the kind of men that go to those places, right?"

Kevin nodded, and Mackenzie saw the first tear slide down his left cheek. She almost reached out and took his hand as a sign of comfort but she didn't want to antagonize him.

"I need you to think about whether or not your mom ever came home really upset or mad about something. I need you to also think about any men that might have…well, any men that might have come home with her."

"No one ever came home with her," he said. "And I hardly ever saw Mom angry or upset about anything. The only time I ever saw her mad was when she was dealing with the lawyers last year."

"Lawyers?" Mackenzie asked. "Do you know why she was speaking with lawyers?"

"Sort of. I know that something happened at work one night and it made her end up talking to some lawyers. I heard bits and pieces of it when she was on the phone. I'm pretty sure she was talking to them about a restraining order."

"And you think this was in regards to where she worked?"

"I don't know for sure," Kevin said. He seemed to have brightened a bit once it seemed that he had said something that might be of assistance. "But I think so."

"That's a huge help, Kevin," Mackenzie said. "Is there anything else you can think of?"

He shook his head slowly and then looked into Mackenzie's eyes. He was trying to remain strong but there was so much sadness in the boy's eyes that Mackenzie had no idea how he hadn't broken down yet.

"Mom was ashamed of it, you know?" Kevin said. "She worked from home some during the day. She was this sort of technical writer, doing websites and stuff. But I don't think she was making much money. She did the other thing to make more money because our dad…well, he split a long time ago. He never sends money anymore. So Mom…she had to take this other job. She did it for me and Dalton and…"

"I know," Mackenzie said, and this time she did reach out to him. She placed her hand on his shoulder and he seemed to be grateful. She could also tell that he wanted to cry quite badly but probably wasn't going to allow himself to do it in front of strangers.

"Detective Porter," Mackenzie said, and he emerged from the other room, glaring at her. "Did you have any further questions?" She shook her head subtly as she asked this, hoping he'd pick up on it.

"No, I think we're good here," Porter said.

"Okay," Mackenzie said. "Again, guys, thank you so much for your time."

"Yes, thanks," Porter said, joining Mackenzie in the living room. "Jennifer, you have my number so if you can think of anything that might help us, don't hesitate to call. Even the smallest detail could prove helpful."

Jennifer nodded and let out a croaky, "Thanks."

Mackenzie and Porter made their exit, walking down a set of wooden steps and into the apartment complex parking lot. When they were a safe distance away from the apartment, Mackenzie closed the distance between them. She could feel the immense anger coming off of him like heat but ignored it.

"I got a lead," she said. "Kevin says that his mother was working toward filing a restraining order against someone at work last year. He said it was the only time he had ever seen her visibly mad or upset about something."

"Good," Porter said. "That means that something good came out of you undermining me."

"I didn't undermine you," Mackenzie said. "I simply saw a situation falling apart between you and the oldest son, so I stepped in to resolve it."

"Bullshit," Porter said. "You made me look weak and inferior in front of those kids and their aunt."

"That's not true," Mackenzie said. "And even if it *was* true, what does it matter? You were talking to those kids like they were idiots that could barely comprehend the English language."

"Your actions were a clear sign of disrespect," Porter said. "Let me remind you that I've been at this job for longer than you've been alive. If I need you to step in to help me, I'll damn well tell you."

"You ended it, Porter," she replied. "It was over, remember? There was nothing left to undermine. You were out the door. That was your call. And it was the wrong call."

They had reached the car now and as Porter unlocked it, he looked over the roof, his eyes blazing into Mackenzie.

"When we get back to the station, I'm going to Nelson and put in a request to be reassigned. I'm done with this disrespect."

"Disrespect," Mackenzie said, shaking her head. "You don't even know what that word means. Why don't you start by taking a close look at how you treat me."

Porter let out a shaky sigh and got in the car, not saying anything else. Deciding not to let Porter's tense mood get the best of her, Mackenzie also got in. She looked back to the apartment and wondered if Kevin had allowed himself to cry yet. In the grand scheme of things, the beef that existed between her and Porter really didn't seem all that significant.

"You wanna call it in?" Porter asked, clearly pissed that he had been overstepped.

"Yeah," she said, taking out her phone. As she pulled up Nelson's number, she couldn't deny the slow satisfaction that was building inside of her. A restraining order placed a year ago and now Hailey Lizbrook was dead.

We got the bastard, she thought.

But at the same time, she also couldn't help but wonder if wrapping this thing up would really be this easy.

CHAPTER SIX

Mackenzie finally arrived home at 10:45, exhausted. The day had been long and draining but she knew that she would not be able to sleep for quite a while. Her mind was too focused on the lead that Kevin Lizbrook had supplied. She'd called the information in to Nelson and he assured her that he'd have someone call the strip club and whatever law firm Hailey Lizbrook had been working with to get her restraining order.

With her mind firing off in hundreds of directions, Mackenzie put on some music, grabbed a beer from the refrigerator, and ran herself a bath. She was typically not fond of baths, but tonight every muscle in her body was wound entirely too tight. As the tub filled with water, she walked through the house and tidied up from where Zack had apparently waited until the last minute to go to work again.

She and Zack had moved in together a little over a year ago, trying to take every possible step they could in their relationship that might prevent marriage for as long as possible. Mackenzie felt that she was ready to get married, but Zack seemed terrified of it. They'd been together for three years now and while the first two of those years had been great, the latter part of their relationship had been based on monotony and Zack's fear of being alone and getting married. If he could stay somewhere in between those, with Mackenzie as his buffer, he'd be happy.

Yet as she picked up two dirty plates from the coffee table and stepped over an Xbox disc on the floor, Mackenzie wondered if maybe she was done being a buffer. More than that, she wasn't even sure she'd marry Zack if he asked her tomorrow. She knew him too well; she had seen a picture of what being married to him would be like and, quite frankly, it wasn't too promising.

She was stuck in a dead-end relationship, with a partner who didn't appreciate her. In the same way, she realized, she was stuck in a job with colleagues who didn't appreciate her. Her entire life felt stuck. She knew changes needed to be made, but they felt too daunting to her. And given her level of exhaustion, she just didn't have the energy.

Mackenzie retired to the bathroom and cut off the water. Waves of steam rolled from the top of the water, as though inviting her in. She undressed, looking at herself in the mirror and becoming even more aware that she had wasted eight years of her life with a man who had no real desire to commit his life to her. She felt that she was attractive in a simple sort of way. Her face was pretty (maybe a bit more so when she wore her hair in a ponytail) and she had a solid figure, if a bit thin and muscular. Her stomach was flat and hard—so much so that Zack sometimes joked that her abs were a bit intimidating.

She slipped into the tub, the beer resting on the small towel table beside her. She let out a deep exhale and let the hot water do its work. She closed her eyes and relaxed as best as she could, but the image of Kevin Lizbrook's eyes returned to her on a constant loop. The amount of sadness in them had been almost unbearable, speaking of a pain that Mackenzie herself had once known but had managed to push far back into her heart.

She closed her eyes and dozed, the image haunting her the entire time. She felt a palpable presence, as if Hailey Lizbrook were in the room with her now, urging her to solve her murder.

*

Zack came home an hour later, fresh off a twelve-hour shift at a local textile plant. Every time Mackenzie smelled the scents of dirt, sweat, and grease on him, it reminded her of how little ambition Zack had. Mackenzie had no issue with the job in and of itself; it was a respectable job made for men that were built for hard work and dedication. But Zack had a bachelor's degree that he had intended to use to land a spot in a master's program to become a teacher. That plan had ended five years ago and he had been stuck in the role of shift manager at the textile plant ever since.

Mackenzie was on her second beer by the time he came in, sitting in bed and reading a book. She figured she'd try to fall asleep around three or so, getting a solid five hours before heading in to work at nine the next morning. She'd never cared much for sleep and had discovered that on nights she got more than six hours, she found herself lethargic and out of sorts the next day.

Zack came into the room in his dingy work clothes. He kicked his shoes off by the side of the bed as he looked her over. She was wearing a tank top and a pair of high-riding bicycle shorts.

"Hey, babe," he said, his eyes taking her all in. "So, this is nice to come home to."

"How was your day?" she asked, barely looking up from her book.

"It was okay," he said. "Then I came home and saw you like *this* and it got a lot better." With that, he crawled onto the bed and

29

directly toward her. His hand went to the side of her face as he angled in for a kiss.

She dropped her book and pulled away at once. "Zack, have you lost your mind?" she asked.

"What?" he said, clearly confused.

"You're absolutely filthy. And not only have I taken a bath, but you're getting dirt and grease and God only knows what else on the sheets."

"Ah, God," Zack said, annoyed. He rolled off of the bed, purposefully covering as much of the sheets as he could. "Why are you such a tight-ass?"

"I'm not a tight-ass," she said. "I just prefer to not live in a pig sty. By the way, thanks for cleaning up after yourself before you left for work."

"Oh, it's so nice to be home," Zack sneered, walking into the bathroom and shutting the door behind him.

Mackenzie sighed and chugged down the rest of her beer. She then looked across the room where Zack's dirty work boots were still on the floor—where they would stay until he put them on tomorrow. She also knew that when she got up in the morning and went into the bathroom to get ready, she'd find his dirty clothes in a pile in the floor.

To hell with it, she thought, returning to her book. She read only a few pages while she listened to the water from Zack's shower in the bathroom. She then set the book aside and walked back into the living room. She picked up her briefcase, carried it into the bedroom, and pulled out the most up-to-date files on the Lizbrook murder she had retrieved from the station before coming home. As much as she wanted to rest, even for a few hours, it would not let her.

She looked through the files, digging for any detail that they might have overlooked. When she was certain that everything had been covered, she once again saw Kevin's tear-filled eyes and it pushed her to look again.

Mackenzie was so enamored with the files that she didn't notice Zack coming into the room. He smelled much better now and, with only a towel around his waist, looked much better, too.

"Sorry about the sheets," Zack said almost absently as he dropped the towel and slid into a pair of boxers. "I'm...I don't know...I just can't remember the last time you actually paid any attention to me."

"You mean sex?" she asked. Surprisingly, she found that she was actually up for sex. It might be just what she needed to finally unwind and get to sleep.

"Not just sex," Zack said. "I mean *any* kind of attention. I get home and you're either already asleep or looking through casework."

"Well, that's *after* I've picked up your crap from the day," she said. "You live like a boy that's waiting for mommy to clean up after him. So yeah, sometimes I jump back into work to forget about how frustrating you can be."

"So it's back to this again?" he asked.

"Back to what?"

"Back to you using work as a way to ignore me."

"I don't use it as a way to ignore you, Zack. Right now I'm more concerned with finding out who brutally killed a mother of two boys than making sure you get the attention you need."

"That right there," Zack said, "is why I'm in no hurry to get married. You're already married to your work."

There were about a thousand remarks she could have spat back at him, but Mackenzie knew there was no point. She knew that he was, in a way, right. Most every night, she found the caseloads she brought home more interesting than Zack. She still loved him, without a doubt, but there was nothing new to him—nothing challenging.

"Good night," he said bitterly as he crawled into bed.

She looked at his bare back and wondered if it was, in some way, her responsibility to give him attention. Would that make her a good girlfriend? Would that make her a better investment for a man that was terrified of marriage?

With the idea of sex now a forgotten impulse, Mackenzie simply shrugged and looked back to the case files.

If her personal life had to melt into the background, then so be it. This life, the life inside the case, felt more real to her anyway.

*

Mackenzie walked into her parents' bedroom, and before she made it through the doorframe, she smelled something that made her seven-year-old stomach buckle. It was a tangy sort of smell, reminding her of the inside of her piggy bank—a smell like the copper of pennies.

31

She stepped into the room and saw the foot of the bed, a bed that her mother had not slept in for a year or so—a bed that looked far too big for just her father.

She saw him there, legs dangling over the side of the bed, arms splayed out as if he were trying to fly. There was blood everywhere: on the bed, on the wall, even some on the ceiling. His head was turned to the right, as if he were looking away from her.

She knew he was dead right away.

She stepped toward him, her bare feet padding down in a splatter of blood, not wanting to get closer but needing to.

"Daddy," she whispered, already crying.

She reached out, terrified, but drawn in like a magnet.

Suddenly, he turned and stared at her, still dead.

Mackenzie screamed.

Mackenzie opened her eyes and looked around the room in a glare of confusion. The case files were in her lap, spread out. Zack was sleeping beside her, his back still to her. She took a deep breath, wiping the sweat from her brow. It was just a dream.

And then she heard the creak.

Mackenzie froze. She looked toward the bedroom door and slowly got out of bed. She'd heard the weak floorboard in the living room creaking, a sound that she had only ever heard when someone was walking in the living room. Sure, she had been asleep and in the midst of a nightmare, but she *had* heard it.

Hadn't she?

She got out of bed and grabbed her service pistol from the top of her dresser where it sat by her badge and small purse. She quietly angled herself around the doorframe and walked out into the hallway. The ambient glow of streetlights filtered in through the living room blinds, revealing an empty room.

She stepped into the room, the gun held in an offensive position. Every gut instinct told her that there was no one there, but she still felt shaken. She *knew* she'd heard the floorboards creaking. She walked to that area of the living room, just in front of the coffee table, and heard it creak.

Out of nowhere, the image of Hailey Lizbrook crossed her mind. She saw the lashes on the woman's back and the prints in the dirt. She shuddered. She looked dumbly down to the gun in her hands and tried to remember the last time a case had ever gotten to her this badly. What the hell had she been thinking? That the killer had been here in her living room, sneaking up on her?

Irritated, Mackenzie headed back to the bedroom. She quietly placed the gun back on top of the dresser and went to her side of the bed.

Still feeling slightly spooked and with the remnants of her dream still floating in her head, Mackenzie lay back down. She closed her eyes and tried to find sleep again.

But she knew it would be a hard time coming. She was plagued, she knew, by the living and the dead.

CHAPTER SEVEN

Mackenzie couldn't remember a time when the station had been so chaotic. The first thing she saw when she walked through the front doors was Nancy rushing down the hallway to someone's office. She'd *never* seen Nancy move so quickly. Beyond that, there were anxious looks on the faces of every officer she passed on her way to the conference room.

It looked like it was going to be an eventful morning. There was a tension in the air that reminded her of the thickness of the atmosphere just before a bad summer storm.

She'd felt some of that tension herself, even before she left her house. She'd gotten the first call at 7:30, informing her that they would be moving on the lead within hours. Apparently, while she'd been sleeping, the lead she had managed to pull out of Kevin had turned out to be a very promising one. A warrant was being acquired and a plan was being put into place. One thing had already been established, though: Nelson wanted her and Porter to bring the suspect in.

The ten minutes she spent in the station was a whirlwind. While she poured a cup of coffee, Nelson was barking orders at everyone while Porter sat solemnly in a chair at the conference table. Porter looked like a pouting child looking for any attention he could get. She knew it must be eating at him that this lead had come from a boy that Mackenzie had spoken with—a boy that he had been prepared to walk away from.

Mackenzie and Porter were given the lead, and two other cars were assigned to fall in behind them to assist as needed. It was the fourth time in her career that she had been tasked with such a takedown, and the rush of adrenaline never got old. Despite the surge of energy coursing through her, Mackenzie remained calm and collected. She walked out of the conference room with poise and confidence, starting to get the feeling that this was now *her* case, no matter how badly Porter wanted it.

On her way out, Nelson approached her and took her softly by the arm.

"White, let me talk to you for a second, will you?"

He led her to the side, guiding her into the copy room before she could answer. He looked around conspiratorially, making sure no one was within hearing distance. When he was sure they were safe, he looked at her in a way that made her wonder if she had done something wrong.

"Look," Nelson said, "Porter came to me last night and asked to be reassigned. I flat out told him no. I also told him he'd be stupid to drop out of this case right now. Do you know why he wanted to be reassigned?"

"He thinks I stepped on his toes last night," Mackenzie said. "But it was clear that the kids weren't responding to him and he wasn't going to try hard to get through to them."

"Oh, you don't have to explain it to me," Nelson said. "I think you did a damn good job with that oldest kid. The kid even told some of the other guys that showed up—including the social services guys—that he really liked you. I just wanted to let you know that Porter is up in arms today. If he gives you any shit, let me know. But I don't think he will. While he's not a big fan of yours, he all but told me that he respects the hell out of you. But that stays between you and me. Got it?"

"Yes, sir," Mackenzie said, surprised at the sudden support and encouragement.

"All right then," Nelson said, clapping her lightly on the back. "Go get our guy."

With that, Mackenzie headed out to the parking lot where Porter was already sitting behind the wheel of their car. He gave her a *what the hell is taking so long* sort of look as she went hurrying to the car. The moment she was in, Porter pulled out of the parking spot before Mackenzie had even closed the door all the way.

"I take it you got the full report on our guy this morning?" Porter asked as he pulled out onto the highway. Two other cars pulled out behind them, carrying Nelson and four other officers as backup if needed.

"I did," Mackenzie said. "Clive Traylor, a forty-one-year-old registered sex offender. Spent six months in prison for assault on a woman in 2006. He currently works at a local pharmacy but he also does some woodwork out of a small shed on his property."

"Ah, you must have missed the last memo Nancy sent out," Porter said.

"Did I?" she asked. "What did I miss?"

"The bastard has several wooden poles cut out behind his shed. Intel shows that they're just about the same size as the one we found out in that cornfield."

Mackenzie scrolled through her e-mails on her phone and saw that Nancy had sent the memo out less than ten minutes ago.

"Sounds like our guy, then," she said.

"Damn right," Porter said. He was speaking like a robot, like he had been programmed to say certain things. He did not look over at her a single time. It was clear that he was pissed, but that was okay with Mackenzie. As long as he put that anger and determination into bringing the suspect down, she couldn't care less.

"I'll go ahead and kick the elephant out of the car," Porter said. "It pissed me off *bad* when you took over last night. But I'll be damned if you didn't work some kind of miracle on that kid. You're sharper than I give you credit for. I'll admit that. But the disrespect…"

He trailed off here, as if he wasn't sure how to finish the statement. Mackenzie said nothing in response. She simply looked ahead and tried to digest the fact that she had just received what could almost be considered compliments from two very unlikely sources in the last fifteen minutes.

She suddenly felt that this could be a very good day. Hopefully, by the end of the day, they'd bring in the man responsible for the death of Hailey Lizbrook and several other unresolved murders over the last twenty years. If that was the reward, she could certainly tolerate Porter's sour mood.

*

Mackenzie looked out and felt depressed as she watched the neighborhoods change before her eyes as Porter drove into the more derelict suburbs of Omaha. Well-to-do subdivisions gave way to low-rent apartment complexes which then faded away into seedier neighborhoods.

Soon enough they reached Clive Traylor's neighborhood, consisting of lower-income houses sitting in mostly dead lawns, punctuated with crooked mailboxes along the street. The rows and rows of houses never seemed to end, each one looking less cared for than the next. She did not know what was more depressing to her: their neglected state, or the numbing monotony.

Clive's block was quiet, and as they turned down it, Mackenzie felt the familiar rush of adrenaline. She sat up involuntarily, readying herself to confront a murderer.

According to the surveillance team who had been watching over the property since 3 AM, Traylor was still at home. He was not due to clock in at work until one o'clock.

Porter slowed their car as he drove further up the street and parked directly in front of Traylor's house. He then looked to Mackenzie for the first time that morning. He looked a little on edge. She realized she must have looked the same. And yet, despite their differences, Mackenzie still felt safe walking into potential danger with him. Sexist hard-ass or not, the man had a seasoned record and knew what he was doing most of the time.

"You ready?" Porter asked her.

She nodded and pulled the mic from the dashboard radio unit.

"This is White," she said into the mic. "We're ready to head in on your word."

"Go," came Nelson's simple reply.

Mackenzie and Porter got out of the car slowly, not wanting to give Traylor any cause for alarm if he happened to look out the window to see two strangers walking up his lawn. Porter took the lead as they walked up the rickety porch steps. The porch was covered in flaked white paint and the shells of countless dead insects. Mackenzie felt herself tensing up, preparing. What would she do when she saw the face of the man who had murdered those women?

Porter pulled open the flimsy screen door and knocked on the front door.

Mackenzie stood beside him, waiting, heart pounding. She could feel her palms begin to sweat.

A few seconds passed before she heard approaching footsteps. There came the clicking of a lock being disengaged, the door opened a little more than a crack, and Clive Traylor looked out at them. He looked confused—and then very alarmed.

"Can I help you?" Traylor asked.

"Mr. Traylor," Porter said, "I'm Detective Porter and this is Detective White. If you have a moment, we'd like to speak with you."

"In regards to what?" Traylor asked, instantly defensive.

"About a crime that was committed two nights ago," Porter said. "We just have a few questions and as long as you answer honestly, we'll be out of your hair in five or ten minutes."

Traylor seemed to consider this for a moment. Mackenzie was pretty sure she knew the train of logic that was chugging through his head. He was a registered sex offender, and any resistance to help the police when they asked for it would raise alarms and maybe even further investigation into Traylor's current activities.

And that was the last thing a man like Clive Traylor wanted.

"Yeah, come on in," Traylor finally said, clearly not pleased with the situation. Still, he opened the door and led them into a house that looked like a college dorm room.

There were books stacked everywhere, empty beer cans strewn here and there, and piles of clothes sporadically placed on any available surface. The place smelled like Traylor had recently burned something on the stove.

He led them into his small living room, and Mackenzie took it all in, analyzing everything at rapid speed to determine if this were the house of a killer. There were more clothes bundled up on the couch and the coffee table was littered with dirty dishes and a laptop. Seeing such disarray made Mackenzie realize that maybe Zack's living habits weren't as bad as she had thought. Traylor did not ask them to have a seat—which was good, because there was no way Mackenzie was going to sit anywhere in this house.

"Thanks for your time," Porter said. "As I said, there was a crime committed two nights ago—a murder. We're here because you have a rather shaky past with the victim."

"Who was it?" Traylor asked.

Mackenzie watched him closely, studying his facial expressions and posture, hoping she'd find some clues there. So far, all she could tell was that he was very uncomfortable having police inside his house.

"A woman named Hailey Lizbrook."

Traylor seemed to think about this for a second and then shook his head.

"I don't know anyone by that name."

"Are you sure?" Porter asked. "We have proof that she placed a restraining order against you last year."

Realization dawned over him and he rolled his eyes.

"Oh. *Her.* I never knew her name."

"But you knew where she lived?" Mackenzie asked.

"I did," Traylor said. "Yeah, I followed her home from the Runway a few times. I had policemen come to my house and talk to me about that. But I haven't gone against that order. I swear it."

"So you don't deny that you stalked her at some point?" Porter asked.

Mackenzie saw the embarrassment flush over Traylor and her heart dropped. She was pretty certain this was not their man.

"No. I'll admit that. But after that restraining order, I stayed away. I even stopped going to that strip club."

"Okay," Porter said. "Can you tell me where you were two nights ago?"

"Well, I worked until nine o'clock and then I came home. I watched some TV and went to bed around midnight."

"Do you have proof of that?" Porter asked.

Traylor looked taken off guard, trying to come up with a suitable answer. "Hell, I don't know. I logged into my bank account online. Can you use that?"

"We can," Porter said, pointing to the laptop on the coffee table. "Show us."

Traylor started wrestling with something in that moment. He slowly reached for the computer but then hesitated. "That's, well, that's a breach of my privacy. Come back with a warrant and I'll—"

"This isn't my first rodeo," Porter said. "We've got more officers outside and I can have them in here within thirty seconds. We already have a warrant. So make this as easy as possible and show me your browsing history."

Traylor was practically sweating now. Mackenzie was pretty sure he was not the murderer, but he was certainly hiding *something*.

"What's the problem?" Mackenzie asked.

"You'll have to get that information directly from my bank," he said.

"Why?"

"Because there's no trace of my history on this computer."

Porter stepped forward and repeated his earlier command. "Show us."

Mackenzie and Porter stood around Traylor, one on each side. Mackenzie watched closely, noticing that Traylor pulled up his browser very quickly. Still, Mackenzie had seen his home screen and was pretty sure she had seen enough.

She stepped away from Traylor as he showed Porter that his search history was at zero. She also listened to him explain to Porter that he always deleted his browsing history to get rid of cookies and junk in his cache. She let Porter discuss this age-old excuse with him while she peeked out into his hallway. There were no pictures on his walls, just clutter on the floor along the walls. Among the mess, she saw an empty box that raised an alarm.

Mackenzie walked back into the living room as the conversation between Porter and Traylor continued to get a little more heated.

"Excuse me," she said, speaking over them. "Mr. Traylor, I don't doubt you. I'm fairly certain you had nothing to do with the murder of Hailey Lizbrook. I will tell you that a lot of factors were pointing to you, right down to the poles behind your shed out back. But no, I don't think you killed anyone."

"Thank you," he spat sarcastically.

"White," Porter said, "what are you—"

"But I *am* going to need you to tell me what other inappropriate things you've been involved in."

He looked surprised, almost insulted. "Nothing," he said. "I know my record isn't stellar. Once you're a registered sex offender, your life never goes back to the way it was. People look at you differently and—"

"Save it, please," Mackenzie said. "Are you sure you haven't been involved in anything you shouldn't?"

"I swear it."

Mackenzie nodded and then looked to Porter with a thin smile. "Detective Porter, would you like to cuff him or should I do it?"

Before he could answer, though, Traylor was on the move. He collided with Mackenzie, trying to knock her down and make his way to the hall. He clearly hadn't been expecting her to be so solid, though. She braced her feet and locked her knees as Traylor rammed into her, causing him to rebound in confusion.

"Shit," Porter muttered, fumbling for his service pistol.

As he scrambled for his gun, Mackenzie threw a hard elbow into Traylor's chest as he tried to pivot around her. He let out a *whoof* and gave her a surprised look. He started dropping to a knee, but before it even touched the floor, Mackenzie grabbed him by the back of the neck and slammed him down to the floor.

Traylor cried out as Mackenzie planted a knee into his back and whipped out her handcuffs like a magician working with handkerchiefs.

"Never mind," Mackenzie said, cutting her eyes at Porter. "I'll do it."

With that, she slapped the cuffs on Traylor's wrists as Porter stood motionless, his hand still frozen by his hip where his gun still remained holstered.

*

Mackenzie looked at the plastic bag and was sickened by what she was pretty sure was on the USB drives inside. There were eleven of them in all. After some harsh interrogation, they'd discovered that these USBs were what Traylor had been going for when he'd made the mistake of trying to dash past Mackenzie.

"Hot damn," Nelson said, looking a bit too happy as Clive Traylor was placed into the back of a police cruiser. "It's not the arrest I wanted today, but I sure will take it."

A little less than an hour had passed since Traylor had denied being involved in anything suspicious. In that hour, his laptop had been confiscated and his history had been recovered. Several USB drives had also been found in the house, filled with photos and videos. With what was found on his computer, including websites visited in the last two days, and the USB drives, Clive Traylor had been in possession of more than five hundred images and twenty-five videos of child pornography. More than that, he was selling the files online. The most recent transaction had been to an IP address in France for a sum of two hundred dollars—a transaction that had been confirmed by Traylor's bank.

Clive Traylor had been nowhere near the cornfield where Hailey Lizbrook had been killed two nights ago. Instead, he had been online, distributing child pornography.

When Mackenzie had seen the icon for incognito browsing software on Traylor's home screen and then the box for IP-blocking hardware in Traylor's hallway, she had been able to put the pieces together. The fact that Traylor was a known sex offender had made the equation all the easier to solve.

Nelson was standing with Mackenzie and Porter while Traylor was driven away.

"We think we just touched the surface of this," he said. "Once we can get past that software he had installed, I think we're going to find a hell of a whole lot more. Damn good work, you two."

"Thanks, sir," Porter said, clearly at odds with taking the praise that Mackenzie mostly deserved.

"By the way," Nelson said, looking directly at Mackenzie now, "I sent some guys to the shed out back. There was nothing there—just some unfinished handmade stuff—a bookshelf, a few tables, things like that. I even had them check the poles behind the shed and it turns out they're made of pine, the same as the stuff he's building. So it was just a huge coincidence."

"I was *sure* this was the guy," Porter said.

"Well, don't let this set you back," Nelson said. "The day is young."

Nelson left them, heading over to speak with the tech crew that was working on getting deeper into Traylor's laptop.

"That was sharp thinking in there," Porter said. "I would have missed both of those things—the software on his computer and the hardware box."

He sounded depressed, almost sad.

"Thanks," Mackenzie said, a little uncomfortable. She wanted to tell him how she had come to her conclusions but figured that would only irritate him. So she kept quiet, as always.

"Well," Porter said, clapping his hands together as if the matter were now totally resolved. "Let's get back to the station and see what else we can dig up on our killer."

Mackenzie nodded, taking her time to get into the car. She looked back to Clive Traylor's house and the shed in the backyard. She could see the ends of the poles from where she stood. On the surface, yes, this had seemed like a sure thing. But now that it had turned out to be something else entirely, she was again faced with the fact that they were pretty much back to square one.

There was still a killer out there and with each minute that passed, they were giving him another chance to kill again.

CHAPTER EIGHT

As a boy, one of his favorite pastimes was to sit out on the back porch and watch their cat stalk around the yard. It was particularly interesting whenever it came upon a bird or, on one occasion, a squirrel. He'd watched that cat spend up to fifteen minutes stalking a bird, toying with it until it finally pounced on it, tearing out its neck and sending its little feathers into the air.

He thought of that cat now, as he watched the woman arrive home from yet another night at work—a place of employment where she stood up on a stage and pandered her flesh. Like that cat from his childhood, he had been stalking her. He'd nixed the idea of taking her at her workplace; the security was tight and even under the murky glare of the early morning streetlights, there was too much of a chance of getting caught. Instead, he'd waited in the parking lot of her apartment complex.

He parked directly in front of the stairs on the far right side of the complex, as those were the ones she used to go to her apartment on the second floor. Then, after three o'clock, he'd climbed those stairs and waited on the landing between the first and second flight of stairs. It was poorly lit and dead quiet at this time of the night. Still, as a decoy, he had an old cell phone that he would quickly place to his ear and pretend to talk into if someone happened to pass him.

He'd followed her for two nights now and knew that she'd get home sometime between three and four in the morning. On both of the occasions where he had followed her and parked on the opposite side of the street, he had only seen one person use those stairs between three and four in the morning, and they had been clearly drunk.

Standing on the landing, he had seen her car pull up and he now watched as she got out. Even dressed in street clothes, she seemed to flaunt her legs. And what had she been doing all night? Showing those legs, making men yearn.

She approached the stairwell and he brought the phone to his ear. A few more steps and she'd be right in front of him. He felt his calf muscles tightening, waiting to spring, and he once again thought of his childhood cat.

Hearing the light sounds of her footfalls below, he started pretending to talk. He spoke quietly but not in a conspiratorial way. He thought he might even give her a smile when she showed up.

And then she was there, coming up around the landing, heading for the second flight of stairs. She glanced at him, saw that he was occupied and looked harmless, and gave him a little nod. He nodded back, smiling.

When her back was to him, he acted quickly.

His right hand went into his jacket pocket, pulling out a rag that he had soaked in chloroform seconds before getting out of the car. He used his other arm to wrap around her neck, dragging her backwards and off of her feet. She was only able to let out a tiny little yelp of surprise before the rag was pressed against her mouth.

She struggled immediately, biting down and somehow managing to dig into his pinky. Her bite was hard and he was sure she had bitten clean through his finger at first. He pulled back for just a moment, but it was enough for her to get away from him, wrenching away from the grip he had applied around her neck with the crook of his left arm.

She started up the stairs and let out a whimper. This whimper, he knew, would evolve into a scream in no time. He dove forward, reaching out and grabbing that silken bare leg. The stairs struck him in the chest and stomach, knocking the wind from him, but he was still able to pull hard at her leg. With a desperate little cry, she went falling to the ground. There was a shuddering *crack* as her face struck the stairs.

She went limp and he instantly crawled up the stairs to get a closer look. She'd struck her temple on the stair. Surprisingly, there was no blood, but even in the weak light, he could tell that a knot was already starting to form.

Moving quickly, he put the cloth back into his pocket, finding that she had gnawed into his pinky pretty good. He then picked her up and found that there was no sturdiness in her legs. She had been knocked out cold.

But he'd dealt with this before, too. He picked her up from the side the knot was forming on and leaned all of her weight on that side. He then dragged her down the stairs with one arm around her waist, her feet dragging uselessly behind her. With his other hand, he brought the dead phone up to his other ear just in case they passed someone in the fifteen feet or so that separated them from his car. He had his lines prepared just in case that happened: *I don't know what to tell you, man. She's drunk—like passed out drunk. I figured it was best to take her back to her house.*

But the late hour didn't necessitate that bit of acting. The stairs and the parking lot were absolutely dead. He got her into his car without incident, never seeing anyone.

44

He cranked his car and pulled out of the parking lot, heading east.

Ten minutes later, as her head knocked softly against the passenger window, she muttered something that he could not understand.

He reached over and patted her hand.

"It's okay," he said. "It's all going to be okay."

CHAPTER NINE

Mackenzie was reading over the final report on Clive Traylor, wondering where she went wrong, when Porter stepped into her office. He still looked a little disgruntled from the morning. Mackenzie knew he'd been sure Traylor had been their guy and he *hated* being wrong. But his constant irritable mood was something Mackenzie had gotten used to a long time ago.

"Nancy said you were looking for me," Porter said.

"Yes," she said. "I think we need to pay a visit to the strip club that Hailey Lizbrook worked at."

"Why?"

"To speak with her boss."

"We've already spoken to him on the phone," Porter said.

"No, *you* spoke to him on the phone," Mackenzie pointed out. "For a grand total of about three minutes, I might add."

Porter nodded slowly. He stepped fully into the office, closing the door behind him. "Look," he said, "I was wrong about Traylor this morning. And you impressed the hell out of me with that takedown. It's clear that I haven't been showing you enough respect. But that still doesn't give you the right to talk down to me."

"I'm not talking down to you," Mackenzie said. "I'm simply pointing out that in a case where our leads are next to zero, we need to exhaust every possible avenue."

"And you think this strip club owner might be the murderer?"

"Probably not," Mackenzie said. "But I think it's worth talking to him to see if he can lead us to anything. Besides that, have you checked the guy's rap sheet?"

"No," Porter said. The grimace on his face made it clear that he hated to admit this.

"He has a history of domestic abuse. Also, six years ago, he was involved with a case where he supposedly had a seventeen-year-old working for him. She came out later on and said she only managed to get the job by performing sexual favors for him. The case was thrown out, though, because the girl was a runaway and no one could prove her age."

Porter sighed. "White, do you know the last time I stepped foot in a strip club?"

"I'd rather not know," Mackenzie said. And by God, did she get an actual *smile* out of him?

"It's been a long time," he said with a roll of his eyes.

"Well, this is business, not pleasure."

Porter chuckled. "When you get to be my age, the line between the two sometimes blurs. Now come on. Let's go. I imagine strip clubs haven't changed *that* much in the last thirty years."

*

Mackenzie had only seen strip clubs in movies and although she hadn't dared tell Porter, she hadn't been sure what to expect. When they walked inside, it was just after six o'clock in the evening. The parking lot was starting to fill with stressed out men coming off of their work shifts. A few of these men gave Mackenzie a little too much attention as she and Porter walked through the lobby and toward the bar area.

Mackenzie took the place in as best she could. The lighting was dim, like a permanent twilight, and the music was loud. Currently, two women were on a runway-like stage, dancing with a pole between them. Wearing only a pair of thin panties each, they were trying their best to dance in a sexy manner to a Rob Zombie song.

"So," Mackenzie said as they waited for the bartender, "has it changed?"

"Nothing except the music," Porter said. "This music is terrible."

She had to give it to him; he wasn't watching the stage. Porter was a married man, going on twenty-five years. Seeing he was focused on the rows of liquor bottles behind the bar rather than the topless women onstage made her respect for him go up a notch. It was hard to peg Porter as a man who respected his wife that much and on such an account, she was happy to be proven wrong.

The bartender finally came over to them and his face went slack right away. While neither Porter nor Mackenzie wore any sort of police uniform, their attire still presented them as people that were there on business—and probably not business of the positive kind.

"Can I help you?" the bartender asked.

Can I help you? Mackenzie thought. *He didn't ask us what he could get us to drink. He asked if he could help us. He's seen our kind in here before. Strike one for the owner.*

"We'd like to speak to Mr. Avery, please," Porter said. "And I'll have a rum and Coke."

"He's busy at the moment," the bartender said.

"I'm sure he is," Porter said. "But we need to speak with him." He then took his badge out of his interior coat pocket and flashed it, returning it back as if he had just pulled off a magic trick. "But he

47

needs to speak to us or I can make some calls and make it *really* official. It's his call."

"One second," the bartender said, not wasting another minute. He walked to the other side of the bar and went through double doors that reminded Mackenzie of the kind she'd seen in saloons in those cheesy Western movies.

She looked back to the stage where there was now only one woman, dancing to Van Halen's "Running with the Devil." There was something about the way the woman moved that made Mackenzie wonder if strippers lacked dignity and therefore did not care about exposing their bodies, or if they were just *that* confident. She knew there was no way in hell she could ever do something like that. While she was confident in many things, her body was not one of them, despite the many lewd glances she received from random men from time to time.

"You look a little out of place," someone beside her said.

She looked to her right and saw a man approaching her. He looked to be about thirty years old and as if he had been sitting at the bar for a while. He had that sort of gleam to his eyes that she'd seen in many a drunken altercation.

"There's a reason for that," Mackenzie said.

"I'm just saying," the man said. "You don't see many women in places like this. And when they *are* here, they're usually here with a husband or boyfriend. And quite frankly, I don't see the two of you," he said, pointing to Porter, "as being an item."

Mackenzie heard Porter chuckle at this. She wasn't sure what annoyed her more: the fact that this man had gotten brave enough to sit beside her or that Porter was enjoying every minute of it.

"We're not an item," Mackenzie said. "We work together."

"Just here for the after-work drinks, huh?" he asked. He was leaning in closer—close enough for Mackenzie to smell the tequila on his breath. "Why don't you let me buy you one?"

"Look," Mackenzie said, still not looking at him. "I'm not interested. So just move along to the next unwitting victim."

The man leaned in closer and stared at her for a moment. "You don't have to be a bitch about it."

Mackenzie turned to him finally and when they locked eyes, something in the man's gaze shifted. He could tell she meant business, but he'd had a few drinks too many and apparently just couldn't help himself. He placed a hand on her shoulder and smiled at her. "I'm sorry," he said. "What I meant to say is, well, no, I meant what I said. You don't have to be a bitch about—"

"Get your hand off of me," Mackenzie said softly. "Last warning."

"You don't like the feel of a man's hand?" he asked, laughing. His hand slid down her arm, groping now rather than simply touching. "I guess that's why you're here to look at naked women, huh?"

Mackenzie's arm came up with lightning speed. The poor drunk man didn't even realize what had happened until after she'd thrust her forearm into his neck and he was falling off of his barstool, gagging. When he hit, it made enough noise to attract one of the security guards that had been standing by the edge of the lounge area.

Porter was then on his feet, stepping in between the guard and Mackenzie. He flashed his badge and, to Mackenzie's surprise, stood nearly toe-to-toe with the much larger guard. "Slow down, big boy," Porter said, all but rubbing the guy's face with his badge. "In fact, if you want to avoid the spectacle of having someone arrested in this seedy establishment, I suggest you toss this jack-off out of here."

The guard looked from Porter to the drunk man on the floor, still coughing and gasping for air. The guard understood the option he was facing and nodded. "Sure thing," he said, hauling the drunk man to his feet.

Mackenzie and Porter watched as the guard escorted the drunk man to the door. Porter nudged Mackenzie and chuckled. "You're just full of surprises, huh?"

Mackenzie only shrugged. When they turned back around to the bar area, the bartender had returned. Another man stood beside him, staring down Mackenzie and Porter as if they were stray dogs that he didn't trust.

"You want to tell me what that was all about?" the man asked.

"Are you Mr. William Avery?" Porter asked.

"I am."

"Well, Mr. Avery," Mackenzie said, "your patrons need to do a better job of keeping their mouths shut and their hands to themselves."

"What's this about?" Avery asked.

"Is there somewhere more private we can speak?" Porter asked.

"No. Here is fine. This is the busiest time of the day for us. I need to be here to help tend bar."

"You sure do," Porter said. "I ordered a rum and Coke five minutes ago and I still haven't seen it."

The bartender scowled and then turned to the bottles behind him. In his absence, Avery leaned forward and said, "If this is about Hailey Lizbrook, I already told your other cop buddies everything I know about her."

"But you didn't talk to me," Mackenzie said.

"So what?"

"So, I take a different approach than almost everyone else, and this is our case," she said, nodding toward Porter. "So I need you to answer more questions."

"And if I don't?"

"Well, if you don't," Mackenzie said, "I can interview a woman named Colby Barrow. That name sound familiar? I believe she was seventeen when she started working here, right? She got the job by performing oral sex on you, I believe. The case is dead, I know. But I wonder if she'd have anything to tell me about your business practices that might have been swept under the rug six years ago. I wonder if she might be able to tell me why you don't seem to give a damn that one of your dancers was killed three nights ago."

Avery looked at her like he wanted to slap her. She almost wanted him to try it. She had encountered far too many men like him in the last few years—men that cared noting for women until the lights were out and they needed sex or something to punch on. She held his gaze, letting him know that she was much more than a punching bag.

"What do you want to know?" he asked.

Before she answered, the bartender finally delivered Porter's drink. Porter sipped from it, smiling knowingly at Avery and the bartender.

"Did Hailey have men that came in and usually flocked to her?" Mackenzie asked. "Did she have regulars?"

"She had one or two," Avery said.

"Do you know their names?" Porter asked.

"No. I don't pay attention to the men that come in here. They're just like any other men, you know?"

"But if it came down to it," Mackenzie said, "do you think some of your other dancers might know their names?"

"I doubt it," Avery said. "And let's face it: most of the dancers ask for the man's name just to be nice. They don't give a shit what their names are. They're just trying to get paid."

"Was Hailey a good employee?" Mackenzie asked.

"Yes, she was, actually. She was always willing to work extra shifts. She loved her two boys, you know?"

"Yes, we met with them," Mackenzie said.

Avery sighed and looked out to the stage. "Listen, you're welcome to talk to any of the girls if you think it will help figure out who killed Hailey. But I can't let you do it here, not right now. It would upset them and screw with my business. But I can give you a list of their names and phone numbers if you absolutely need it."

Mackenzie thought about this for a minute and then shook her head. "No, I don't think that will be necessary. Thanks for your time, though."

With that, she got up and tapped Porter on the shoulder. "We're done here."

"I'm not," he said. "I still need to finish my drink."

Mackenzie was about to argue her point when Porter's phone rang. He answered it, pressing his free hand to his other ear to block out the godawful noise of the current Skrillex song blaring from the PA. He spoke briefly, nodding in a few places before hanging up. He then downed the remainder of his drink and handed the car keys to Mackenzie.

"What is it?" she asked.

"It seems I *am* done," he said. Then his face became set. "There's been another murder."

CHAPTER TEN

They drove a little over two and a half hours from the strip club after receiving the call, night falling slowly the entire way, increasing Mackenzie's depressed mood, and when they arrived at the scene, night had fallen. They finally turned off the main highway onto a strip of unpaved blacktop, and then onto a dirt road that led to a large open field. As they neared their destination, she started to feel an impending sense of doom.

Her headlights glowed just ahead of her as she carefully drove down a bumpy dirt track, and slowly, she started to see the numerous police cars already on the scene. A few of them were pointed to the center of the field, their headlights revealing a grisly, yet familiar sight.

As much as she tried not to, she flinched at the sight.

"My God," Porter said.

Mackenzie parked, but never took her eyes from the scene as she stepped out of the car and walked slowly forward. The grass in the field was high, coming to her knees in places, and she could see the slightly worn trail that the officers had been using. There were too many officers here; she already worried that the scene was contaminated.

She looked up and took a sharp breath. It was another woman, stripped to her underwear, bound to a pole that looked to be roughly eight feet tall. This time, seeing the woman strung up in such a way, Mackenzie was unable to repress a memory of her sister. Steph had been a stripper, too. Mackenzie wasn't exactly sure what Steph was up to these days, but it was too easy to imagine her ending up like this.

As Mackenzie approached the victim, she glanced around the crime scene and counted seven officers in all. Two officers were off to the side, speaking with two teenagers. Up ahead, standing a few feet away from the pole and the victim, Nelson was speaking with someone on his phone. When he saw them, he waved them over and quickly ended his call.

"Anything of substance from the strip club?" Nelson asked.

"No sir," Mackenzie said. "I'm convinced Avery is clean. He's offered the names and numbers of all of his employees if we need them, but I don't think we'll need his help."

"We need *someone's* help," Nelson said, looking to the pole and looking as if he might get sick.

Mackenzie approached the body and saw right away that this one was in worse shape than the body of Hailey Lizbrook. For starters, there was a large lump and bruise on the left side of the woman's face. There was also dried blood in and around her ear. The lashes on her back looked to have been made with the same weapon, only this time they had been applied with more force and in greater succession.

"Who discovered the body?" Porter asked.

"Those two kids over there," Nelson said, pointing toward where one of the officers was still speaking to the two teens. "They admitted they came out here to make out and smoke some weed. They say they've done it for a month or so. But tonight, they found this."

"Same body type as Hailey Lizbrook," Mackenzie said, thinking out loud. "I think we can probably assume the same profession, or similar, too."

"I need answers on this, you two," Nelson said. "And I need them *now*."

"We're trying," Porter said. "White is on fire with this thing and—"

"I need results," Nelson said, close to fury. "White, I'll even take some of your out-of-the-box thinking on this one."

"Can I borrow a flashlight?" she asked.

Nelson reached into his coat pocket and took out a small Maglite which he happily tossed to her. She caught it, flicked it on, and started looking around the scene. She tuned out Nelson's nervous banter and let him release his steam with Porter.

With the dead-on precision that took over her in moments like this, the world melted away as she started scouring the scene for any clues. There were several that stood out right away. For instance, she knew that Nelson and the other officers had used the same beaten path to get to the body to prevent contaminating the scene; outside of their worn-down footpath from their cars to the body, there were several other indentations in the tall grass, likely placed there by the killer.

She strayed a bit outside of the footpath and slowly arced the flashlight beam around the field surrounding the post. She took some mental notes, looked back over to the two teens, and then headed back to the pole. She looked the body over for any further clues and became certain that this body, like that of Hailey Lizbrook, would show no signs of sexual abuse.

She wondered if setting up the pole was more than just a theatrical device. Something about it seemed resolute, almost like a necessity for the killer. For a brief moment she could see him, his hands falling on the pole and going to work.

He drags it with pride, maybe even hoisting it up along his back. There's labor to the task, a prerequisite to the killings. Struggling with the pole, bringing it to the site, digging the hole and installing it—there's a sweat-of-the-brow satisfaction in it. He is readying the site for the murder. He takes just as much satisfaction from this work as he does the murder.

"What are your thoughts, White?" Nelson asked as he watched her circle the body.

Mackenzie blinked, being torn from the image of the killer in her mind. Realizing just how deep she'd gone there for a moment, she felt a slight chill pass through her.

"A few easy ones right off the bat are that you can see the trail where he dragged the pole from the dirt track to here," she said. "That concludes that the pole was not here originally. He brought it with him. And that denotes that he drives either a pickup truck or a van of some kind."

"That's what I figured," Nelson said. "Anything else?"

"Well, it's hard to be sure at night," she said, "but I'm pretty sure the killer had the victim wrapped in something when he brought her out here."

"Why's that?"

"I don't see any blood at all on the grass but some of the wounds on her back—especially those around her buttocks—are still fairly wet."

As Nelson digested this, Mackenzie went to her haunches at the back of the pole and pressed the grass down with one hand. With the other, she shone the flashlight beam along the bottom of the pole.

Her heart raced as saw the numbers: N511/J202.

He uses a knife or a chisel, and he takes a lot of time and effort to make sure the carvings are legible. These carvings are important to him and, more than that, he wants them to be seen. Whether consciously or subconsciously, he wants *someone to figure out why he's doing this. He needs someone to understand his motives.*

"Chief?" she said.

"Yeah, White?"

"I've got those numbers again."

"Shit," Nelson said, coming to where she was kneeling. He looked down and let out a heavy sigh. "Any idea what they mean?"

"None at all, sir."

54

"Okay," Nelson said. His hands were on his hips and he was looking up to the dark sky like a man defeated. "So we have a few more answers here, but nothing that's going to tie things up for us anytime soon. A man driving a truck or van that has access to wooden poles and—"

"Wait," Mackenzie said. "You just said something."

She went back to the rear of the pole. She leaned down to look at the place where the woman's wrists were bound with rope.

"What is it?" Porter asked, coming over to have a look.

"You any good with knots?" she asked.

"Not really."

"I am," Nelson said, also coming over to have a look. "What have you got?"

"I'm pretty sure this is the same knot that was used for Hailey Lizbrook."

"So what if it is?" Porter said.

"It's a bit unusual," Mackenzie replied. "Can you tie a knot like that? I can't."

Porter looked at it again, seeming stumped.

"I'm pretty sure it's a sailor's knot," Nelson said.

"I thought so," Mackenzie said. "And while it might be a long shot, I'd consider that our killer might be familiar with boats. Maybe he lives near the water or *has* lived near the water at some point."

"Drives a truck or a van, maybe lives near water, and has some sort of mommy issues," Nelson said. "Not much to go on, but it's better than where we were yesterday."

"And given the ritualistic manner of these killings," Mackenzie said, "and the short time frame between the two, we can only assume he's going to do it again."

She turned and looked at him, summoning all the seriousness she could.

"With all due respect, sir, I think it's time we call in the FBI."

He frowned.

"White, their processes alone would slow us down. We'd have two more bodies before they even sent anyone out here."

"I think it's worth a try," she said. "We're getting in over our heads."

She hated to admit it but the look on Nelson's face showed her that he agreed. He nodded solemnly and looked back to the body on the pole. "I'll make the call," he finally said.

From behind them, they heard a very punctuated curse from one of the other officers. They all turned to see what was going on and saw the bouncing glow of headlights coming down the dirt road.

"Who the hell is that?" Nelson asked. "No one else should know about this and—"

"A news van," said the officer who had let out a curse.

"How?" Nelson said. "Dammit, who the hell keeps getting information to these assholes?"

The scene became a flurry of activity as Nelson did everything he could to prep for the arrival of a news crew. He was fuming and looked like his head might explode at any moment. Mackenzie took the opportunity to take as many photos as she could: of the depressed sections of the field, of the knot at the victim's wrists, of the numbers at the bottom of the post.

"White, Porter, get out of here and get back to the station," Nelson said.

"But sir," Mackenzie said, "we still need to—"

"Just do as I say," he said. "You two are the leads on this case and if the media gets a whiff of that, they'll constantly be on your asses and slow you down. Now get out of here."

It was a sensible train of thought and Mackenzie did as she was asked. But as she headed back to the car with Porter, another thought occurred to her. She turned back to Nelson and said: "Sir, I think we should have the wood tested, on this pole and the last one. Get a sample and have it analyzed. Maybe the kind of wood being used for these posts could lead us to something."

"Damn good thinking, White," he said. "Now haul ass."

Mackenzie did just that as she saw two more pairs of headlights trailing in behind the first set. The first set belonged to a news van with WSQT written on the side. It had just parked on the far side of the police cars. A reporter and a cameraman came bustling out and Mackenzie instantly thought of them as vultures circling a fresh kill.

As she got into the car, taking the driver's seat again, another member of the news crew got out of the van and started snapping pictures. Mackenzie was mortified to see that the camera was pointed in her direction. She lowered her head, got into the car, and started the engine. As she did, she saw that three officers were already storming toward the news van, Nelson in the center. Still, the reporter did her best to bully her way forward.

They took off, but Mackenzie knew it was already too late.

Come tomorrow, her picture would be on the front page of all the papers.

CHAPTER ELEVEN

As it turned out, Nelson had been wrong about the FBI. Mackenzie got the call at 6:35 in the morning requesting that she drive to the airport to pick up an agent that had flown in. She'd had to hurry, as the flight arrived at 8:05, and was embarrassed that she'd have to make a first impression without even having time to fix her hair.

Her hair, though, was the least of her concerns as she sat in the uncomfortable airport chair, waiting at the gate. She was pounding down a cup of coffee, hoping to push her mind beyond caring that her body had only managed five hours of sleep the night before. It was her third cup of the morning and she knew she'd get the jitters if she didn't slow down. But she couldn't afford to be tired and sloppy.

She reviewed everything in her head as she waited for the agent to get off the plane, recircling the gruesome scene from the night before. She couldn't help but feel as if she had missed something. Hopefully, the FBI agent would be able to help get them on a clearer path.

Nelson had e-mailed her the agent's dossier, which she had read quickly while eating a breakfast of a banana and a bowl of oatmeal. Because of this, Mackenzie spotted the agent right away as he stepped off the jet bridge and into the airport. Jared Ellington, thirty-one years old, a Georgetown graduate with a background that included a stint in profiling in counterterrorism cases. His black hair was slicked back as it had been in his picture and the telltale suit he wore painted him as someone on official duty.

Mackenzie walked across the gate to meet him. She hated the fact that she kept going back to her stupid hair. She felt frazzled and out of sorts, having been rushed earlier in the morning. More than that, she had never really cared much about first impressions and had never been the sort of person to worry too much about her appearance. So why now?

Maybe it was because he was from the FBI, an agency she revered. Or maybe it was because, despite herself, she was struck by his looks. She hated herself for that, not only because of Zack, but because of the urgent and gruesome nature of their work.

"Agent Ellington," she said, extending her hand, forcing her tone to be as professional as possible. "I'm Mackenzie White, one of the detectives on the case."

"Good to meet you," Ellington said. "Your chief tells me you're the lead detective on the case. Is that right?"

She did her best to hide her shock but nodded.

"That's correct," she said. "I know you just got off the plane, but we need to hurry and get you to the station."

"Of course," he said. "Lead the way."

She led him through the airport and back out to the parking lot. They were silent during the walk and Mackenzie took the time to size him up. He seemed a little relaxed, not stiff and rigid like the few Bureau guys she'd encountered. He also seemed very serious and intense. He had a much more professional air than any of the men she worked with.

As they drove onto the interstate, fighting through morning airport traffic, Ellington started scrolling through a series of e-mails and documents on his phone.

"Tell me, Detective White," he said, "what sort of person do you think we're looking for? I've looked through the notes that Chief Nelson sent me and I have to say that you seem pretty sharp."

"Thanks," she said. Then, quick to dismiss the compliment, she added: "As for the type of person, I'm thinking it stems from abuse. When you consider that the victims were not sexually abused, yet stripped to their underwear, it indicates that these are murders based on some need for revenge on some woman that wronged him earlier in life. So I think it might be a man that is embarrassed by sex or, at the very least, finds it gross."

"I see you have not ruled out religious contexts," Ellington said.

"No, not yet. The very nature of how he displays them has obvious crucifixion overtones. Plus the fact that the women he's killing are all representations of male lust makes it hard to rule out."

He nodded, still scrolling through his phone. She cast glances in his direction as she made her way through traffic and was struck by how handsome he was. It wasn't obvious at first, but there was something very plain yet rugged about Ellington. He'd never be a leading man but would make an attractive addition to the hero's team.

"I know this seems rude," he said, "but I'm trying to make sure I'm well-versed in this. As I'm sure you know, I was called in on this case less than six hours ago. It's been a whirlwind."

"No, not rude at all," Mackenzie said. She found it refreshing to be in a car with a man and not have the conversation be filled with sideways insults and sexism. "Do you mind if I ask what your initial thoughts on the killer are?"

58

"My big question is why he displays the bodies at all," Ellington said. "It makes me think the murders aren't just out of some personal vendetta. He wants people to see what he's done. He wants to make a spectacle out of these women, which denotes that he's proud of what he's doing. I'd go so far as to guess that he feels he's doing the world a favor."

Mackenzie felt a stirring of excitement as they neared the precinct. Ellington was the polar opposite of Porter and seemed to have the same sort of approach to profiling as she did. She couldn't remember the last time she had been able to freely share her thoughts with a co-worker without fear of being ridiculed or spoken down to. Already, she could tell that Ellington was easy to talk to and valued the opinions of others. And, quite frankly, it didn't hurt that he was nice to look at.

"I feel like you're on the right track," Ellington said. "Between the two of us, I think we can nail this guy. Looking at the information about the knots, the fact that he drives a van or truck, and apparently uses the same weapon each time, there's a lot to go on. I look forward to working with you on this, Detective White."

"Likewise," she said, catching another glimpse of him out of the corner of her eye as he continued to dutifully read through e-mails on his phone.

Her excitement continued to bloom; she felt a sense of motivation she had not felt toward her work in a very long time. She felt inspired, reinvigorated—and that things were about to change in her life.

*

A little over an hour later, Mackenzie was quickly brought back to reality as she watched Agent Jared Ellington stand in front of a conference room filled with local police that clearly felt like they didn't need his help. A few sitting around the table were taking notes, but there was a tension in the air that showed on everyone's face. She noticed that Nelson sat near the head of the conference table, looking nervous and uncomfortable. It had ultimately been his call to contact the FBI and it was clear that he wasn't sure if it had been the right choice.

Meanwhile, Ellington did his best to keep control of the room as he went through a short spiel where he went over the same material that he and Mackenzie had discussed on the way from the airport—that they were looking for a killer that likely had some aversion to sex and was also proud of the murders. He also went through a review of all of the clues they had to go on and what they might mean. It wasn't until he got to the topic of having the wood from the posts analyzed that he got any sort of response from the officers scattered round the table.

"In regards to the wood samples," Nelson said, "we should have results from that within a few hours."

"What good would that do, anyway?" Porter asked.

Nelson looked over to Mackenzie and nodded, giving her permission to field that question. "Well, based on the results, we could look into local logging companies or mills to see if anyone has recently purchased that certain type of post."

"Seems like a long shot," an older cop in the back of the room said.

"It does," Ellington said, quickly taking back control of the room. "But a long shot is better than no shot at all. And please, make no mistake about it; I am not here to assume total control over this case. I'm just here as a moving part of the solution, a point-man to make sure you have full access to any resources the Bureau can provide. That includes research, manpower, and anything else to help bring this killer in. I'm here only temporarily—probably no more than thirty-six or forty-eight hours—and then I'm gone. This is your show, guys. I'm just the hired help."

"So where do we start?" another cop asked.

"I'll be working with Chief Nelson following this briefing to divide you up as appropriate," Ellington said. "We'll have a few of you head out to speak with Hailey Lizbrook's co-workers. And as I understand it, we'll have fully autopsy results and information on the deceased discovered last night. As soon as we have a positive ID, some of you will need to visit her family and friends to mine for information. We'll also need someone to check with local mills when we get the results of the wood test back."

Again, Mackenzie noticed the stiff posture of most of the police around the table. She found it hard to believe they were so proud (or perhaps, she thought, too lazy) to take direct orders from someone that they did not know well, regardless of his place in the food chain. Was small-town mentality that hard to break away from? She'd often wondered this in the midst of the demeaning way most of the men in this room had treated her since she arrived.

"That's all I have for now," Ellington said. "Any questions?"

Of course, there were none. Nelson, however, got to his feet and joined Ellington at the front of the room.

"Agent Ellington will be working with Detective White, so if you need him, you can find him in her office. I know this is a little unorthodox, but let's take it for what it is and take full advantage of the Bureau's generosity."

There were mumbles and grumbles of acknowledgment as officers got up from the table and headed out on their way. As they filed out, Mackenzie noticed that a few of them were looking at her with more reproach and angst than usual. She looked away as she got up and joined Nelson and Ellington at the front of the room.

"Is there something I should know?" Mackenzie asked Nelson.

"What do you mean?"

"I'm getting nastier looks than usual," she said.

"Nasty looks?" Ellington asked. "Why do you usually get nasty looks?"

"Because I'm a determined younger woman who speaks her mind," Mackenzie said. "Men around here don't care for that. There are a few that think I should be home, in the kitchen."

Nelson looked highly embarrassed, and a little pissed, too. She thought he might actually say something to defend himself and his officers, but he didn't get a chance. Porter joined them and slapped the day's local newspaper down on the table.

"I think *this* is the reason for the dirty looks," he said.

They all looked down to the paper. Mackenzie's heart grew cold as Nelson let out a curse behind her.

The front page headline read "SCARECROW KILLER STILL AT LARGE." Under that, the subtitle read: "Beleaguered police force seems to have no answers as another victim is discovered."

The picture beneath it showed Mackenzie getting into the car she and Porter had driven out to the field yesterday. The photographer had captured the entire left side of her face. The hell of it was that she looked rather pretty in the picture. Whether she wanted to admit it or not, this picture placed directly beneath the headline essentially painted her as the face of the investigation.

"That's not fair," she said, hating the way it sounded coming out of her mouth.

"The guys think you're getting off on it," Porter said. "They think you're bent on breaking this case for the publicity."

"Is that how *you* feel?" Nelson asked him.

Porter took a step back and sighed. "Personally, no. White has proven herself to me over these last few days. She wants this guy captured, no matter what."

"Then why don't you stand up for her?" Nelson said. "Run some interference while we wait for the latest victim to be ID'd and for the results on that wood sample."

Looking like a child that had just been scolded for lying, Porter put his head down and said, "Yes, sir." He made his exit without looking back.

Nelson looked back down to the paper and then at Mackenzie. "I say you make the most of it. If the media wants to put a pretty face to this investigation, let them run with it. It'll make you look that much better when you bring this bastard in."

"Yes, sir."

"Agent Ellington, what do you need from me?" Nelson asked.

"Just your best detective."

Nelson grinned and hitched a thumb toward Mackenzie. "You're looking at her."

"Then I think we're good."

Nelson headed out of the conference room, leaving Ellington and Mackenzie alone. Mackenzie started to gather up her laptop and notes while Ellington looked around the room. It was clear that he felt out of place and wasn't sure how to handle it. She was a little out of place herself. She was glad everyone else was gone. She enjoyed being alone with him; it made her feel as if she had a confidant in all of this, someone who saw her as an equal.

"So," he said, "they really look down on you because you're young and a woman?"

She shrugged.

"Seems that way. I've seen rookies come in—men, mind you— that get some ribbing, but they aren't spoken down to the way they speak down to me. I'm young, motivated, and, according to a few, not too bad to look at. Something about that combination throws them off. It's easier for them to write me off as the over-ambitious piece of ass than a woman under thirty years of age that has a harder work ethic than them."

"That's unfortunate," he said.

"I've felt a slight shift in the last few days," she said. "Porter in particular seems to be coming around."

"Well, let's wrap this case up and bring them all around," Ellington said. "Can you arrange to have every photo from both sites brought into your office?"

"Yeah," she said. "Meet me there in about ten minutes."

"You got it."

Mackenzie decided right there and then that she liked Jared Ellington a little too much for her own good. Working with him for the next few days would be challenging and interesting—but for reasons other than the case at hand.

CHAPTER TWELVE

Mackenzie got home just after seven that night, knowing full well that she could be called at any moment. There were so many avenues open now, so many different leads that could potentially require her attention. She could feel her body getting tired. She had not been sleeping well since visiting the first murder scene and she knew that if she didn't allow herself time to rest, she'd end up making clumsy mistakes while at work.

When she walked through the door, she saw Zack sitting on the couch with an Xbox controller in his hand. A bottle of beer was on the coffee table in front of him, with two empties lined up in the floor. She knew he'd had the day off and assumed this was how he'd spent it. It made him look like an irresponsible child in her eyes and it was *not* what she wanted to see after coming in from a day like today.

"Hey, babe," Zack said, barely looking away from the television.

"Hey," she said dryly, heading for the kitchen. Seeing the beer on the coffee table, she had the urge to enjoy one. But honestly, feeling exhausted and on edge, she decided on a cup of peppermint tea instead.

As she waited for the kettle to boil, Mackenzie walked into the bedroom and changed clothes. She had overlooked dinner and was suddenly faced with the fact that there was very little in the house to eat. She hadn't been grocery shopping in a while and she knew damn good and well that Zack hadn't thought to do it.

When she had changed into gym shorts and a T-shirt, she walked back out to the enticing whistle of the tea kettle. As she poured the water over the bag, she heard the muted gunfire from Zack's game. Curious and wanting to at least broach the topic to see how he'd respond, she was unable to keep her frustration to herself.

"What did you do for dinner?" she asked.

"Haven't eaten yet," he said, not bothering to look away from the television. "Were you going to make something?"

She glared at the back of his head and, for a moment, wondered what Ellington was doing. She doubted that *he* played videogames like some loser locked in his childhood. She waited a moment, letting her rage pass, and then took a step into the living room.

"No, I'm not making anything. What have you been doing all afternoon?"

She could hear his sigh even over the explosions from the game. Zack paused the game and finally turned to look at her. "And just what in the hell is that supposed to mean?"

"It was just a question," she said. "I asked what you had been doing this afternoon. If you hadn't been playing your little game, maybe you could have made dinner. Or at the very least picked up a pizza or something."

"I'm sorry," he said, sarcastically and with volume. "How am I supposed to know when you're going to get home? You never communicate that stuff with me."

"Well, call and ask," she snapped.

"What the hell for?" Zack asked, dropping the controller and getting to his feet. "The few times I *do* bother calling you at work, the call goes straight to your voicemail and you never call me back."

"That's because I'm *working,* Zack," she said.

"I work, too," he said. "I bust my ass at that damn factory. You have no idea how hard I work."

"Yes, I do," she said. "But tell me this: when was the last time you saw me just sitting on my ass? I come home and I'm usually faced with your dirty clothes on the floor or dirty dishes in the sink. And you know what, Zack? I work hard, too. I work *damn* hard and I have to see shit on a day-to-day basis that would make you crumble. I don't need to come home to a little boy playing video games and asking what we're having for dinner."

"*Little boy?*" he asked, nearly shouting now.

Mackenzie hadn't meant to go that far, but there it was. It was a plain and simple truth she'd been holding in for months now and now that it was out, she felt relieved.

"That's how it seems sometimes," she said.

"You bitch."

Mackenzie shook her head and took a step back. "You have three seconds to take that back," she said.

"Oh, go to hell," Zack said, coming around the couch and approaching her. She could tell he wanted to get in her face, but he knew better than to do that. He knew that she could easily take him in a fight; it was something that he had no problem telling her whenever he vented about things that made him unhappy in their relationship.

"Excuse me?" Mackenzie asked, almost hoping that he'd get aggressive and get in her face. And as she felt that, she felt something else with absolutely clarity: their relationship was over.

"You heard me," he said. "You're not happy, and neither am I. It's been that way for a while, Mackenzie. And quite frankly, I'm tired of putting up with it. I'm tired of coming second and I *know* I can't compete with your work."

She said nothing, not wanting to say anything else to provoke him. Maybe she'd get lucky and this argument would be over soon, bringing them to the end they both wanted without an extensive knock-down-drag-out fight.

In the end, all she said was, "You're right. I'm not happy. Right now, I have no time for a live-in boyfriend. And I certainly don't have time for arguments like this one."

"Well then, sorry to waste your time," Zack said quietly. He picked up his beer bottle, gulped down what remained in it, and set it hard on the table—so hard that Mackenzie thought the glass might break.

"I think you should leave for now," Mackenzie said. She held eye contact with him, holding his gaze so he'd know this was non-negotiable. They'd had fights in the past where he'd *almost* packed his things and left. But this time, it needed to happen. This time, she'd make sure there were no apologies, no makeup sex, no manipulative conversations about how they needed each other.

Zack finally looked away from her and when he did, he looked furious. Still, he made sure to leave a few inches between them when he stomped past her and toward the bedroom. Mackenzie listened to him go, standing in the kitchen and idly stirring her tea.

So this is what I've become, she thought. *Alone, cold, and emotionless.*

She frowned, hating the inevitability of it all. She'd once had a mentor who had warned her about this—how if she pursued a career in law enforcement with high ambition, her life would become too busy and hectic for anything resembling a healthy relationship.

After a few minutes, Mackenzie heard Zack start muttering to himself. As drawers in the bedroom opened and closed, she heard the terms *fucking bitch, work obsessed,* and *heartless fucking robot.*

The words hurt (she didn't try to pretend to be so hardened that they didn't), but she shrugged them off. Instead of focusing on them, she started cleaning up the mess Zack had accumulated during the day. She cleaned up empty beer bottles, a few dirty dishes, and a pair of dirty socks as the man who had created the mess—a man she had, at one time, fallen in love with—continued to curse and call her names from the bedroom.

*

Zack was gone by 8:30 and Mackenzie was in bed an hour later. She checked her e-mail, seeing a few reports flying back and forth between Nelson and other officers, but there was nothing that needed her immediate attention. Satisfied that she might actually get a handful of uninterrupted hours of sleep, Mackenzie cut off her bedside lamp and closed her eyes.

Experimentally, she reached out and felt the empty side of the bed. Having Zack's side of the bed empty wasn't too jarring because he was often not there when she went to sleep because of his work shifts. But now, knowing that he was gone for good, the bed seemed much larger. As she stretched out and felt that empty side of the bed, she wondered when she had fallen out of love with him. It had been at least a month, she knew that for sure. But she'd said nothing in the hopes that whatever had existed between them might resurface.

Instead, things had gotten worse. She often thought that Zack had sensed her becoming more distant as her feelings had died down. But Zack was not the type to acknowledge such a thing. He avoided conflict at all costs and, as much as she hated to admit it, she was pretty sure he would have stuck around for as long as possible just because he feared change and was too lazy to move out.

As she sorted through all of these things, her cell phone rang. *Great,* she thought. *So much for sleep.*

She switched her lamp back on, fully expecting to see Nelson's or Porter's number on her display. Or maybe it would be Zack, calling to ask her if he could please come back. Instead, she saw a number she did not recognize.

"Hello?" she said, doing her best not to sound tired.

"Hi, Detective White," a man's voice said. "This is Jared Ellington."

"Oh, hi."

"Did I call too late?"

"No," she said. "What's up? Do you have something new?"

"No, I'm afraid not. In fact, I got word tonight that we won't have the results on that wood until morning."

"Well, at least we know how the day will start," she said.

"Exactly. But listen, I was wondering if you could meet me for breakfast," he said. "I'd like to go over the case details with you. I want to make sure we're on the same page and not missing even the smallest detail."

"Sure," she said. "What time do you—"

66

She stopped here, looking toward her bedroom door.

For a split second, she'd heard something move out there. Once again, she'd heard that damned floorboard creak. But more than that, she'd heard a shuffling sound. Slowly, she got out of bed, still holding the phone to her ear.

"White, you still there?" Ellington asked.

"Yes, I'm here," she said. "Sorry. I was asking what time you'd want to meet."

"How about seven o'clock at Carol's Diner? You know it?"

"I do," she said, walking to the doorway. She looked out and saw only shadows and dark, muted outlines. "And seven sounds good."

"Great," he said. "I'll see you then."

She barely heard him as she stepped out of her bedroom and into the small hallway that led to the kitchen. Still, she managed to get out a "Sounds good," before hanging up.

She cut on the hallway light, revealing the kitchen and making the living room look murky. Just like several nights ago, there was no one there. But, just to make sure, she walked into the living room and cut on the light.

Of course, there was no one there. The room offered no places to hide and the only thing unchanged about it was the missing Xbox that Zack had taken with him. Mackenzie looked around the room one more time, not liking the fact that she had spooked so easily. She even walked across the creaky board, testing its noise and comparing it to what she had heard.

She checked the lock on the front door and then headed back to her bedroom. She looked back behind her one more time before cutting out the lights and returning to sleep. Before she turned her lamp off, she took her service pistol out of the bedside drawer and placed it on top, within arm's reach.

She looked at it in the gloom of the bedroom, knowing that she'd not need it but feeling safer that it was right there, in plain sight.

What was happening to her?

CHAPTER THIRTEEN

"Daddy? Daddy, it's me. Wake up."

Mackenzie stepped into the bedroom and braced herself, turning from the sight of her dead father.

"What happened, Daddy?"

Her sister was in the room, too, standing on the other side of the bed, looking at their father with a disappointed look on her face.

"Steph, what happened?" Mackenzie asked.

"He called out for you and you didn't come. This is your fault."

"No!"

Mackenzie stepped forward again and then, knowing it was lunacy to do so, she still crawled onto the bed and snuggled up next to her father. Soon, she knew, his flesh would be cold and pale.

Mackenzie woke with a start, the nightmare jarring her awake at 3:12 AM, matted in sweat. She sat there, breathing hard, and despite herself, she started to cry.

She missed her dad so much that it hurt.

She sat there, alone, crying herself to sleep.

But it would be hours, she knew, before she fell back asleep. If at all.

In a strange way, she yearned to throw herself back into the case. Somehow, that was less painful.

*

When Mackenzie arrived at Carol's Diner a few hours later, she was awake and alert. Looking across a small diner table at Agent Ellington, the idea of how much her nightmare had affected her, of how easily she had gotten spooked last night, was embarrassing. What in the hell was wrong with her?

She knew what it was. The case was getting to her, stirring up old memories she thought she had laid to rest. It was affecting the way she lived. She'd heard of this happening to others before but had never experienced it herself until now.

She wondered if Ellington had ever experienced it. From her side of the table, he looked well-polished and professional—the spitting image of what Mackenzie expected an FBI agent to be. He was well built but not massive, confident but not cocky. It was hard to imagine him being rattled by much of anything.

68

He caught her looking and rather than looking away embarrassed, she held his gaze.

"What is it?" he asked.

"Nothing, really," she said. "I'm just wondering what it's like to know that with a single phone call, you can get the Bureau looking into something that it would take me several hours to convince the local PD to look into."

"It's not always that smooth," Ellington said.

"Well, with this case, the Bureau seems motivated," Mackenzie pointed out.

"The ritualistic set-up of the murder scenes practically screams serial killer," he said. "And now, with another body discovered, it seems that's exactly what we have."

"And has Nelson been accommodating?" she asked.

Ellington smiled and it showed signs of a subtle charm lurking under his finely composed exterior. "He's trying to be. Sometimes the small-town mentality is hard to break out of."

"Don't I know it," Mackenzie said.

The waitress came by to take their orders. Mackenzie opted for a veggie omelet while Ellington ordered a huge breakfast platter. With that distraction over, Ellington clasped his hands together and leaned forward.

"So," he said. "Where do we stand on this?"

Mackenzie knew he was giving her a chance to show him how she worked. It was in his tone and the slight smile that barely touched the edges of his mouth. He was ruggedly handsome and Mackenzie was slightly uncomfortable with how often her eyes were drawn to his mouth.

"We have to wait on the leads for now and really study them," she said. "The last time we had what we thought was a promising lead, we were dead wrong."

"But you busted a guy that was selling kiddie porn," Ellington pointed out. "So it wasn't a total waste."

"That's true. But still, I'm going to assume you've noticed the hierarchy of our local PD. If I don't figure this out soon, I'll be stuck in my position for a very long time."

"I'm not so sure about that. Nelson thinks highly of you. Whether or not he'd admit it to the other guys, well, that's a different story. That's why he has me helping you. He knows you can get this done."

She looked away from him for the first time. She wasn't sure how she'd get this case wrapped up if she didn't stop jumping at every little sound in her house and sleeping with her gun on the nightstand.

"I figure we start with the wood sample," she said. "We visit whoever is the local supplier of that sort of wood, right down to how it's sawed. If that doesn't produce anything, we're going to have to really start grilling the women that Hailey Lizbrook worked with. We may even have to get as desperate as to look through security cameras from the club she worked at."

"All good ideas," he said. "Another idea I'm going to pitch to Nelson is to have undercover officers on site at some of the strip clubs within a one-hundred-mile radius. We can pull some agents from the Omaha office if we need to. Looking back through old cases—which, I must say, you nailed right on the head during an earlier meeting according to Nelson—we may also be on the lookout for a man that's pursuing prostitutes as well. We can't just assume it's strippers."

Mackenzie nodded, even though she was beginning to doubt that the case she had recalled from the '80s where a prostitute had been strung from a line pole was related to this case. Still, it was nice to have her efforts acknowledged by someone with experience.

"Okay," Ellington said. "So I have to ask."

"Ask what?"

"It's clear that you're undermined at the local level. But it's also clear that you bust your ass and know your stuff. Even Nelson has told me that you're one of his most promising detectives. I had a look at your records, you know. Everything I saw was impressive. So why stay here where you're sneered at and not given a fair chance when you could easily be working as a detective anywhere else?"

Mackenzie shrugged. It was something she had asked herself multiple times and the answer, while morbid, was simple. She sighed, not wanting to get into it but, at the same time, did not want to pass up the opportunity. She'd spoken about her reasons for staying local with Zack a few times—back when they had still been communicating—and Nelson knew some of her history as well. But she could not remember the last time someone had willingly invited her to speak about it.

"I grew up just outside of Omaha," she said. "My childhood was…not the best. When I was seven years old, my father was killed. I was the one that discovered the body, right there in his bedroom."

Ellington frowned, his face filled with compassion.

"I'm sorry," he said softly.

70

She sighed.

"He was a private investigator," she added. "He'd been a beat cop for about five years before that, though."

He sighed, too.

"It's my theory that at least one out of every five cops has some sort of unresolved trauma from their past that is related to a crime," he said. "It's that trauma that made them want to protect and serve."

"Yeah," Mackenzie said, not sure how to respond to the fact that Ellington had just sized her up in less than twenty seconds. "That sounds about right."

"Was your father's killer ever found?" Ellington asked.

"No. Based on the case files I've read and the little bit my mother has told me about what happened, he had been investigating a small group that dealt in smuggling drugs in from Mexico when he was killed. The case was pursued for a while but was dropped within three months. And that was that."

"Sorry to hear it," Ellington said.

"After that, when I realized that there was a lot of lazy, sloppy work in the justice system, I wanted to do something in law enforcement, to be a detective, to be exact."

"So you achieved your dream by the age of twenty-five," Ellington said. "That's impressive."

Before she could say anything else, the waitress came by with her food. She set the plates out and as Mackenzie started to dig in on her omelet, she was surprised to see Ellington close his eyes and say a silent grace over his food.

She couldn't help but stare for a moment as his eyes were closed. She had not thought of him as a religious man and something about seeing him pray over his food touched her. She stole a glance at his left hand and saw no wedding ring. She wondered what his life was like. Did he have a bachelor pad with beer stocked in the fridge, or was he more of the type to have a wine rack and IKEA bookshelves lined with classic and modern literature?

She was working with an open book here. More interesting was how he had become an FBI agent. She wondered what he was like in an interrogation room, or in the heat of the moment when guns were drawn and a suspect was within a hair of either surrendering or opening fire. She knew none of these things about Ellington—and that was exciting.

When he opened his eyes and started eating, Mackenzie looked away, back to her food. After a moment, she couldn't help herself.

"Okay, so how about you?" she asked. "What led you to a career with the FBI?"

"I was a child of the eighties," Ellington said. "I wanted to be John McClane and Dirty Harry, only with more refinement."

Mackenzie smiled. "Those are pretty good role models. Dangerous, but risky."

He was about to say something else when his cell phone rang.

"Excuse me," he said, reaching into his jacket pocket and pulling out the phone.

Mackenzie listened in to his side of the conversation, which turned out to be short. After a few affirmative responses and a quick *Thanks*, he killed the call and looked forlornly at his food.

"Everything okay?" she asked.

"Yeah," he said. "We're going to need to box this up, though. The results from the wood sample came in."

He looked right at her.

"The lumber yard it originated from is less than half an hour away."

CHAPTER FOURTEEN

Mackenzie had always loved the smell of freshly cut wood. It went back to Christmas holidays spent with her grandparents after her father had died. Her grandfather had heated his house with an old wood stove and the back end of the house had always smelled of cedar and the not entirely unpleasant smell of fresh ash.

She was reminded of that old wood stove as she stepped out of the car and into the gravel lot of Palmer's Lumber Yard. To her left, a saw mill was set up, running a huge tree down a belt and toward a saw that was roughly the size of the car she had just stepped out of. Beyond that, several piles of freshly downed lumber waited its turn for the saw.

She took a moment to watch the process. A loader that looked to be a mix of a small crane and a toy-grabbing machine lifted the logs and deposited them onto an archaic-looking machine that pushed them into a belt. From there, the logs were led directly to a saw which she assumed was adjusted for each log by a mechanism or control panel that she could not see from where she sat. As she turned away from this, she saw a truck going out of the lumber yard's exit with a trailer of crudely cut timber stacked about twelve feet high.

Oddly enough, she thought of Zack as she watched it all. He had applied to work at a place like this on the other end of town right around the time he'd landed the job at the textile mill; when he'd discovered the rotating shifts available at the mill, he'd taken it, hoping for more time off. She thought he might have been good working with lumber; he'd always had a knack for building things.

"Looks like hard work," Ellington said.

"Ours is pretty rough, too," she said, happy to have the thoughts of Zack out of her head.

"That it is," Ellington agreed.

In front of them, a basic concrete building was identified only by black stenciled letters over the front door reading OFFICE. She walked alongside Ellington to the front door and was once again taken aback when Ellington opened the door for her. She didn't think she'd ever been shown such a display of chivalry or respect from anyone on the force since the first day she'd carried a badge.

Inside, the noise from outside was muffled to a dull roar. The office consisted of a large counter with rows of filing cabinets behind it. The smell of cut wood permeated the place and there seemed to be dust everywhere. A single man stood behind the counter, writing something in a ledger as they entered. When he regarded them, it was clear that he was a bit confused—probably by Ellington's suit and Mackenzie's business-casual attire.

"Hey there," the man behind the counter said. "Can I help you?"

Ellington took the lead, which Mackenzie was fine with. He'd shown her the utmost respect and had more experience than she did. It made her wonder where Porter was. Had Nelson kept him back at the office to go over the photos? Or was he on interview detail, maybe speaking with Hailey Lizbrook's co-workers?

"I'm Agent Ellington, and this is Detective White," Ellington said. "We'd like to speak with you for a moment about a case we're trying to wrap up."

"Um, sure," the man said, clearly still confused. "Are you sure you have the right place?"

"Yes, sir," Ellington said. "While we can't reveal the full details of the case, what I can tell you is that a pole has been found at each of the scenes. We took a sample from the wood and our forensics team led us here."

"Poles?" the man asked, looking surprised. "Are you talking about the Scarecrow Killer?"

Mackenzie frowned, not liking the fact that this case was already becoming a staple of public conversation. If a lonely man in a lumber yard office had heard about it, the chances were good that news of the case was spreading like wildfire. And among it all, her face was plastered to newspapers featuring the story.

Indeed, he looked her over, and she thought she could see recognition in his face.

"Yes," Ellington said. "Have you had anyone out of the ordinary come by to purchase these poles?"

"I'd be happy to help you," the man behind the counter said. "But I'm afraid it's going to be something of a rabbit trail for you. See, I only receive and sell lumber from companies or smaller wood yards. Anything that leaves here is usually going to another lumber yard or to a company of some sort."

"What sort of companies?" Mackenzie asked.

"It depends on what kind of wood we're talking about," he said. "The majority of my wood goes to construction companies. But I also have a few clients that are into wood crafting for things like furniture."

"How many clients run through here in the course of a month?" Ellington asked.

"Seventy or so on a good month," he said. "But the last few months have been pretty slow. So it might be easier to find what you're looking for."

"One more thing," Mackenzie said. "Do you place any sort of markings on lumber that goes out of here?"

"For larger orders, I'll sometimes place a stamp on one piece per load."

"A stamp?"

"Yeah. It's done by a small press I have outside. It puts the date and the name of my lumber yard on the piece."

"But nothing engraved or carved?"

"No, nothing like that," the man said.

"Would you be able to pull up the records on which clients have brought pre-cut cedar poles?" Ellington asked.

"Yes, I can do that. Do you know what size?"

"One moment," Ellington said, reaching for his phone, presumably to pull up the information.

"Nine feet," Mackenzie said, pulling the figure from memory.

Ellington looked over to her and gave her a smile.

"One foot underground," Mackenzie said, "and eight feet above the surface."

"The poles were also rather old," Ellington said. "The wood was not fresh. Our tests indicate it had never seen any sort of treatment, either."

"That makes it a little easier," the man said. "If it came from here, older wood would have come out of my scrap stock. Give me a few minutes and I can get you that information. How far back do you need to go?"

"Let's go three months, just to be safe," Ellington said.

The man nodded and went to one of the ancient-looking filing cabinets sitting behind him. As they waited, Mackenzie's cell phone started to ring. When she answered it, she was deathly afraid that it might be Zack calling to request some sort of reconciliation. She was relieved to find that it was Porter.

"Hello?" she said, answering the call.

"Mackenzie, where are you right now?" Porter asked.

"I'm with Ellington at Palmer's Lumber Yard checking on the test results from the chip we took from the pole."

"Any results?"

"It looks like another lead to several other leads."

"Well shit," Porter said. "I hate to tell you, but it doesn't get any better." He hesitated for a minute and she heard a shaky sigh on the other end before he added:

"We've got another body."

CHAPTER FIFTEEN

When they arrived at the new crime scene forty minutes later, Mackenzie was more than a little uneasy that this one was closer to home. The scene was exactly thirty-five minutes from her house, in the backyard of a ramshackle house that had been abandoned long ago. She could practically feel the shadow of this newly murdered woman stretching across the flat land, across the city streets, and falling across her front door.

She did her best to hide her frazzled nerves as she and Ellington walked toward the pole. She looked toward the old house, particularly into its empty window frames. To her, they looked like huge looming eyes, peering out and mocking her.

There was a small crowd of officers around the pole, Porter standing in the center of them. He regarded Mackenzie and Ellington as they approached the pole, but Mackenzie barely noticed. She was too busy taking in the sight of the body, noticing two very distinct differences about this victim right away.

First, this woman had small breasts, whereas the previous two victims had been well-endowed. Second, the lashes that had previously been on the other victims' backs could also be seen on this woman's stomach and chest.

"This is getting out of hand," Porter said, his voice soft and haggard.

"Who discovered the body?" Mackenzie asked.

"The land owner. He lives two miles to the east. He had a chain up on the private dirt road and he just happened to notice it was cut. He says no one comes down here, except an occasional hunter during deer season, but as you know, deer season is several months away. And besides, he says he knows all the men that hunt here."

"Is it a private road?" Mackenzie asked, looking back to the dirt road they had just taken to get here.

"Yes. So whoever did *this,*" he said, nodding at the hung body, "cut the chain down. He knew where he was going to come to show off his next trophy. He preplanned this."

Mackenzie nodded. "That shows willful intent and purpose rather than just some unhinged psychological need."

"Is there any chance the land owner is involved?" Ellington asked.

"I've got two men questioning him at his home right now," Nelson said. "But I doubt it. He's seventy-eight years old and limps when he walks. I can't see him hailing poles around *or* successfully luring strippers into his truck."

Mackenzie stepped closer to the body, Ellington following suit. This woman looked considerably younger than the others—maybe in her early twenties. Her head hung low, looking to the ground, but Mackenzie made note of the dark red lipstick, smeared around her cheek and chin. Her dark mascara had also run, leaving dark streaks down her face.

Mackenzie started around to the back of the pole. The lashes were the same as the other two. Some were still fresh enough to offer a wet edge, the blood not quite dry yet. She hunkered down to the bottom of the pole but was stopped by Nelson.

"I already checked," he said. "Your numbers are there."

Ellington joined her and hunkered down for a look. He looked up at Mackenzie. "No clue what these numbers represent?"

"Nothing," she said.

"I think this goes without saying," Nelson said, "but this case is now going to take top priority over everything. Agent Ellington, how soon can we get some more bodies on this?"

"I can make a call and probably have a few more out here by this afternoon."

"Do it, please. Any results from the lumber yard?"

"We got sixteen names," Mackenzie said. "Most of them are construction companies. We have to check each one and see if they can offer any useful information."

"I'll get some men on it," he said. "For right now, I need you and Ellington chasing down the more promising leads. You two are the point men on this thing, so do whatever the hell you need to do to get it wrapped up. I want this sick fucker sitting in an interrogation room by the end of the day.

"Meanwhile, I'm going to have my men go over maps of the surrounding hundred miles or so. We'll split it up and start staking out isolated areas like this one, the field from the last murder, and cornfields that are easily accessed."

"Anything else?" Ellington asked.

"Nothing I can think of. Just keep me posted on even the smallest detail you might come across. I'll talk with you more about that in a second," Nelson said. He then looked over to Mackenzie and gave her a nod of the head, toward the right. "White, can I talk to you for a second?"

Mackenzie stepped away from the post and followed Nelson off to the side of the dilapidated house, wondering what this was about.

"Are you comfortable working with Ellington?" he asked.

"Yes sir. He's been on point and incredibly helpful in terms of talking things out."

"Good. Look, I'm not an idiot. I know your potential and I know that if there's anyone under my employ that can bring this bastard in, it's you. And I'll be damned if I'm going to just let the feds swing in and take it from us. So I want you working with him. I've spoken with Porter already and reassigned him. He's still on the case, but I've got him helping with the door-to-door stuff."

"And he was okay with that?"

"That's not for you to worry about. For now, you just stick to this case and go with your gut. I'm trusting you to make the right decisions; you don't need to check in with me on every little thing. Just do what you need to do to end this. Can you do that for me?"

"Yes, sir."

"I thought so," Nelson said with a little smile. "Now you and Ellington get the hell out of here and bring us some results."

He gave her a gentle clap on the back which, all things considered, was nearly the equivalent of Ellington opening the door for her at the lumber yard. It was a huge stretch coming from Nelson and she appreciated it. They walked back to the body together and Mackenzie looked back at the numbers. She felt that there was something there, that the key to cracking this whole thing lay in those damned numbers.

A part of him, she sensed, wanted to get caught. He was baiting them.

"You okay?" Ellington asked, standing on the other side of the pole.

She nodded, getting to her feet.

"Have you ever been on a case like this before?"

"Just two," he said. "One of them resulted in eight murders before we caught him."

"Do you think that'll happen here?" she asked.

She hated that the questions made her sound uncertain and maybe even inexperienced, but she had to know. All she had to do was remember how frightened she had been for several minutes in her own home, spooked at what had likely been an imagined sound of a creaking floorboard, to understand just how much this case was starting to affect her. She'd lost a boyfriend, she was slowly losing her cool, and she'd be damned if she'd lose anything else as a result of it.

"Not if we can help it," Ellington answered. He sighed. "So tell me, what do you see here that's new?"

"Well, the fact that the killer chose a road in the middle of nowhere seems odd. The chain across the road didn't stop him. Not only that, but he *knew* it would be there. He was prepared to cut it down."

"Meaning what?"

She knew that he was testing her, but he was doing it in a way that was not insulting her intelligence. He was challenging her, and she was thoroughly enjoying it.

"Meaning that the areas he's choosing aren't just random. He has chosen them for a reason."

"So not just the murders are predetermined, but the locations as well."

"Seems like it. I think I—" she said, but then stopped.

To the right, at the edge of the thin forest, she saw movement.

For a moment, she thought she'd imagined it.

But then she saw it again.

Something was moving, heading deeper into the woods. She could make out just enough of the shape to see that it was a human figure.

"Hey!"

It was all she could think to say and it came out a bit excited. At the sound of her voice, the shape took off even faster, any attempt at stealth now gone as they snapped branches and rustled foliage while they escaped.

Acting on instinct, Mackenzie took off toward the woods at a sprint. By the time Ellington had caught on and followed behind her, Mackenzie was already out of the yard and in the woods. The trees around her seemed just as forgotten and colorless as the house that sat behind her, its black windows still gazing out at her.

She slapped branches away as she ran through the woods. She could just make out the sound of Ellington following behind her but she didn't waste her time or effort looking back.

"Stop!" she demanded.

She wasn't surprised when the figure continued to run. Mackenzie had estimated within a matter of seconds that she was faster than her objective, closing in with a quickness that she had always prided herself on. She caught a few branches to the face and felt cobwebs clinging to her skin but she blasted through the forest, undaunted.

As she closed in on the figure, she saw that it was a man dressed in a black hooded sweatshirt and a pair of dark jeans. Because he did not fully look back a single time, Mackenzie couldn't tell how old he was, but she *could* tell that he was slightly overweight and apparently a little out of shape. She could hear him wheezing as she closed in on his heels.

"Dammit," she said as she reached him, stretching out her arm and grabbing him by the shoulder. "I said *stop*!"

With that, she gave him a hard push which sent him down to the ground. He rolled once before skidding to a stop.

I got him, Mackenzie thought.

The man tried to get to his feet but Mackenzie delivered a swift kick to the back of his knee that sent him down again. He banged his face on a tree root as he fell.

Mackenzie planted a hard knee into the man's back and reached for her weapon. Ellington finally arrived and he also pinned the man to the ground. Now that Ellington's full weight was on him, he'd stopped wriggling. Mackenzie reached to her belt and retrieved her handcuffs, while Ellington pulled the man's arms behind his back to yet another cry of pain. Mackenzie slapped the cuffs on and then pulled the man roughly to his feet.

"What's your name?" Mackenzie asked.

She stepped in front of him and saw him for the first time. The guy looked harmless, overweight and probably in his late thirties.

"Aren't you supposed to ask me things like that *before* you assault me?"

Ellington shook him a bit and applied some pressure to his shoulder. "She asked you a question."

"Ellis Pope," the man said, visibly shaken.

"And why are you here?"

He said nothing at first and in the silence, Mackenzie heard more commotion in the woods. This noise came from her right and when she turned in that direction, she saw Nelson and three other officers come scrambling through the thin trees and foliage.

"What the hell is going on?" Nelson shouted. "I saw you two take off in my rearview and—"

He stopped when he saw the third person with them, his hands cuffed behind his back.

"He says his name is Ellis Pope," Mackenzie said. "He was hanging out at the edge of the forest, watching us. When I called out to him, he went running."

Nelson got in Pope's face and it was clear that Nelson was struggling not to physically assault him. "What were you doing here, Mr. Pope?" Nelson asked. "Did you stay close by to admire your handiwork?"

"No," Pope said, now more frightened than ever.

"Then why were you here?" Nelson asked. "It's the only time I'll ask you before I start to lose my cool."

"I'm a reporter," he said.

"For which paper?" Mackenzie asked.

"No paper. A website. *The Oblong Journal*."

Mackenzie, Nelson, and Ellington shared an uncomfortable glance before Mackenzie slowly reached into her pocket for her phone. She pulled up her browser, searched for *The Oblong Journal*, and opened up the page. She quickly navigated to the Staff page and not only did she find the name Ellis Pope, but the picture in the bio was clearly the same man that stood before him.

It was rare that Mackenzie cursed, but she handed her phone to Nelson and let out a strained, *"Fuck."*

"Now," Ellis Pope said, realizing that he was slowly gaining control of the situation. "Which one of you pigs do I have to talk to about pressing charges?"

CHAPTER SIXTEEN

Mackenzie felt a little out of her element in Ellington's company and oddly enough, it was a feeling that was only magnified as they sat side by side in a bar two hours later. She knew they both looked tired and a little worn, making them fade into the rest of the patrons. They were not the only ones dressed relatively nicely; people coming in off of work were also dressed slightly above casual, pulling up to the bar in the shirts and ties and pantsuits they had worn to work. Dim afternoon light spilled in from the two windows along the other side of the bar but it was the neon behind the bar and the reflection of the overheads from the shelved liquor bottles behind the bar that set the mood.

"Any idea how Pope found out about the scene so quickly?" Ellington asked her.

"None. There has to be a mole on the force."

"That's what I figure," Ellington said. "And because of that, I don't see how Nelson can be too hard on you. There's no way you could have even suspected that the movement in the woods was a journalist. Especially not when Pope took off running like that."

"Let's hope so," she said.

Mackenzie knew she'd gotten off easy. Her superior had watched her take a chubby and defenseless online journalist to the ground in a pretty harsh tackle. And while Pope had gotten nothing more than a slight gash on his temple from falling on a root, and while he had been trespassing on private property, it was still grounds for punishment. Still, she'd gotten what basically equated to a slap on the wrist. She'd seen Nelson dish out much worse for less. It made her wonder, though, just how much faith he had in her. To let her go on her merry way while Ellis Pope was likely making phone calls spoke volumes about his confidence in her.

Of course, he had also demanded that she get the hell out of his sight and go somewhere to re-orient herself before she assaulted the next poor bastard that just happened to get in her way. Sensing a small window of escape before he could think better of his decision to keep her actively on the case, she'd done exactly that.

As she was sipping as responsibly as possible on a locally brewed stout from the tap, she tried to remember the last time she had come to a bar as a means of escaping the world. She'd usually used work for that—something that was much easier to admit to herself now that Zack was out of the picture. But now that work had sent her away for a bit, it felt surreal to be sitting at a bar.

It was stranger still to be sitting next to an FBI agent she had only met yesterday. In the short span of time she'd spent with Agent Ellington, she had figured out a few things about him. First, he was an old-fashioned gentleman: he opened doors for her, always asked her opinion before making a decision, referred to those older than him as ma'am and sir, and he also seemed to be protective over her. When they had come into the bar, two men had made very little effort to hide the fact that they were checking her out. Noticing this, Ellington had stepped beside her, blocking her from their view.

"You know why the men on your force are so hateful toward you, right?" Ellington said.

"I assumed it was just the way they were raised," Mackenzie said. "If I'm not in an apron bringing them a sandwich or beer, what good am I?"

He shrugged. "That could be some of it, but no, I think it's something else. I think it's because you intimidate them. More than that, I think they sort of fear you. They're afraid you might make them look stupid and inept."

"How do you figure?"

He only smiled at her for a moment. And although there was nothing overtly romantic about the smile, it was nice to be looked at in such a way. She couldn't remember the last time Zack had looked at her like that—as something to be appreciated rather than used or tolerated.

"Well, let's get the obvious out of the way: you're young and you're female. You're essentially the brand new computer that's coming into the office to take all of the jobs. You're also a walking encyclopedia for forensics and investigation from what I hear. Throw in the way you chased down that poor journalist today, and it's the complete package. You're the new breed and they're the old dogs. That sort of thing."

"So it's a fear of progress?"

"Sure. I doubt they would ever see it like that, but that's what it boils down to."

"I'm assuming this is a compliment?" she asked.

"Of course it is. This is the third time I've been paired with a highly motivated detective and you're by far the most accomplished and driven I've seen. I'm glad we got paired up."

She only nodded because she wasn't sure how to handle his compliments and evaluations yet. On the job, he'd been very professional and by the book—not only in his approach to the job, but also in the way he had approached her. But now that he was being a little less reserved, Mackenzie was having a hard time drawing the line between where on-duty Ellington stopped and where off-duty Ellington began.

"Did you ever think about joining the Bureau?" Ellington asked.

The question stunned her so badly that she was unable to answer for a moment. Of course she had thought of it. She had once dreamed of it as a child. But even as a determined twenty-two-year-old with her sights on a career in law enforcement, the FBI had seemed like some unattainable dream.

"You have, huh?" he asked.

"Is it that obvious?"

"A little. You looked embarrassed just now. It makes me think that you *have* thought about it but never chased it down."

"It was a dream of sorts that I had for a while," she said.

It was embarrassing to admit it, but there was something about the way that he was reading her that made her not mind as much.

"You've got the skills," Ellington said.

"Thanks," she said. "But I think my roots here are too thick. I feel like it's too late."

"It's never too late, you know."

He looked at her, professional and intense.

"Would you like me to put in a word for you and see if it lands on any interested ears?"

She was blown away by his offer. On the one hand, she wanted to, more than anything; on the other, it brought up all her old insecurities. Who was she to qualify to work for the FBI?

Slowly, she shook her head.

"Thank you," she replied. "But no."

"Why not?" he asked. "Not to talk too badly about the men you work with, but you're being misused."

"What would I do at the FBI?" she asked.

"You'd make a stellar field agent," he said. "Hell, maybe a profiler, too."

Mackenzie looked thoughtfully into her beer, a bit taken aback. She had again been stunned to silence and now felt that she had a lot to consider. What if she could make it as an agent? How drastically would her life change? How rewarding would it be to work a job she loved without the hindrances of men like Nelson and Porter to hold her back?

"You okay?" Ellington asked.

Still peering into the dark beer in front of her, she sighed. She thought about Zack for a moment and could not recall the last meaningful conversation they'd had. When was the last time he'd built her up in the same way Ellington was right now? For that matter, when was the last time *any* man had spoken so highly of her directly in front of her?

"I'm fine," she said. "I appreciate everything you're saying. You've given me a lot to think about."

"Good," Ellington said softly, not missing a beat. "But let me ask you: do you have a history of holding yourself back?"

"I don't think it's my self," she said. "I think it's just...I don't know. My past, maybe?"

"Your dad's death?"

She nodded.

"That's some of it," she said.

There's also my string of failed relationships, she thought, but didn't think it was appropriate to say. And as she dwelled on it, she suddenly wondered if the two were related—her dad's death and her relationships. Maybe the source of all of it was, after all, the death.

Would she ever recover from it? She didn't see how she could. No matter how many bad guys she put behind bars, nothing ever seemed to help.

He nodded as if he understood perfectly.

"I understand," he said.

Then, flashing him a smile so he'd know she was joking, she asked: "Are you psychoanalyzing me, Agent Ellington?"

"No, I'm talking to you. I'm listening. Nothing more."

Mackenzie finished her beer and slid the glass to the edge of the bar. The bartender grabbed it right away and filled it again, placing it back in front of her.

"I know that's why this case has me shaken so badly," she added. "A man is using women. Maybe it's not for sex, but he's inflicting pain and shame on them as a way to express some deranged point."

"And this is the first case you've had like this?"

"Yes. I mean, I've been to domestic dispute calls where a husband roughed up his wife, and I've questioned two women after they were raped. But nothing like this."

She drank from her beer, realizing that it was going down far too easily. She had never been a big drinker and this beer—her third of the night—was pushing her to a line that she had tried to avoid crossing ever since college.

"I don't know if my hunches mean anything to you," Ellington said, "but this guy will be caught within a few days. I'm pretty sure of it. He's getting too cocky and one of these leads we keep accumulating will eventually pay off. Plus, the fact that you're heading it all up is a big plus."

"How can you be so sure?" she asked. "About my performance, I mean? And why are you being so nice?"

He was filling her with confidence and, at the same time, reinforcing a trait she possessed that she knew was one of the worst things about her. She knew she tended to get defensive around men that complimented her, mainly because it always meant they wanted one thing. Looking at Ellington as he smiled her, she didn't think it would be too bad if he was looking for that one specific thing. In fact, she was starting to think she might enjoy the hell out of it. Of course, he was going back tomorrow and the chances were very good that she'd never see him again.

Maybe that's exactly what I need, she thought. *One night. No emotion, no expectations, just the dark and this too-good-to-be-true FBI agent that seems to know all the right things to say and—*

She shut the thought down because, quite frankly, it was far too enticing. She then realized that Ellington had still not answered her question: *Why are you being so nice?*

He bit back his smile and finally answered.

"Because," he replied, "you deserve a break. I got my position because a friend knew a friend who knew a deputy chief. And I can guarantee you that half of the cavemen on your force can say the same thing or something similar."

She laughed, and the sound of it made her realize that she was just about to tip over that line. As she tried to recall the last time she had gotten drunk, she tipped back the rest of her beer and slid the glass to the edge of the bar. When the bartender came for it, she shook her head.

"Can you drive?" she asked. "I'm a bit of a lightweight. Sorry."

"Yeah, that's fine."

When the bartender came over with their tabs, Ellington quickly picked hers up before she could lay a hand on it. Watching him do that, she decided that she was going to find out what one emotionless night with a man straight out of a dream might be like. After all, she now had her house and her bed all to herself. What could it hurt?

They walked outside to the car and she noticed that Ellington was walking extremely close to her. He opened her car door for her, furthering his charm in her eyes. When he closed the door and walked around to the driver's side, Mackenzie rested her head against the headrest and took a deep breath. From an abandoned house with a dead woman on a pole to here, on the verge of propositioning a man she had only met yesterday—had this really all happened in the course of less than twelve hours?

"Your car is at the station, right?" Ellington asked.

"It is," she said. And then, her heart beating, she hesitantly added, "But we pass my place on the way—we could just stop there if you want."

He gave her a perplexed look and the corners of his mouth seemed to battle between a smile and a frown. It was clear that he knew what she was suggesting; she didn't doubt he'd had similar offers before.

"Ah, Jesus," he said, rubbing at his head. "To further show you my strong will and character, this is the part where I tell you I'm married."

Mackenzie looked to his left hand—the same hand she had glanced at several times in the bar just to make sure. There was no ring there.

"I know," he said. "I never wear it when I'm working. I hate the way it feels when I have to go for my gun."

"Oh my God," Mackenzie said. "I'm—"

"No, it's okay," he said. "And believe me, I'm beyond flattered. I meant everything I said in there. And while I'm sure the primal male in me will mentally kick my ass for this for the rest of my life, I love my wife and my daughter very much. I think I—"

"Can you just take me to my car?" Mackenzie asked, embarrassed. She looked out of the window and felt like screaming.

"I'm sorry," Ellington said.

"Don't be. It's my fault. I should have known better."

He started the car and pulled out of the lot. "Better than what?" he asked as they headed back for the station.

"Nothing," she said, still refusing to look at him.

But in the silence that hung heavy on the way to the station, she thought: *I should have known better than to believe in something too good to be true.*

As they drove home in the silence, she wanted to curl up in a ball and die, hating herself, wondering if she had just blown the best opportunity to come along in her life in a long, long time.

CHAPTER SEVENTEEN

Mackenzie woke at 6:45 the following morning to the sound of an incoming text. She was already awake, dressed in her underwear. She checked the message and her heart dropped to see it was from Ellington.

Heading home. I'll call you later today to check in.

She thought about calling him right then and there. She was well aware that she'd acted like an immature jilted teenager yesterday. Hell, she hadn't really even been rejected. Ellington had simply stayed true to his character, adding *faithful husband* to his long list of admirable characteristics.

In the end, she let it go. She still felt embarrassed but more than that, she felt defeated. And that was not something she felt very often. The killer was still out there and they were no closer to catching him than they had been three days ago. She'd lost her live-in boyfriend of three years and then found herself infatuated with an FBI agent less than twenty-four hours later. To make matters worse, she'd seen a promise of what her future could be when she was with Ellington; she had seen what her job could be like with someone that respected her and, in a way, was in awe of her. And now that was gone.

She had only Porter and Nelson to look forward to, surrounding her with doubt in the midst of a case that was getting under her skin.

As she slid a shirt on, she sat on the corner of her bed and looked at her cell phone. Suddenly, it was not Ellington that she wanted to call. She was thinking of someone else—someone else who shared the same traumas and sense of failure that she knew so well.

With a sudden pit in her stomach, Mackenzie picked her cell phone up from the dresser and scrolled through her contacts. When she reached the name Steph, she pressed CALL and then nearly ended it right away.

By the time the phone started ringing, she already regretted making the call. It rang twice on the other end before it was answered. The voice of her sister on the other end was familiar, but one she didn't hear nearly enough.

"Mackenzie," Stephanie said. "It's early."

"You never sleep past five," Mackenzie pointed out.

"That's true. But I was just making a point. It's early."

"Sorry," she said. It was a word she used a lot when she spoke to Steph. Not because she actually meant it, but Steph had a way of heaping on the guilt in an effortless way about the smallest of things.

"What did Zack do this time?" Steph asked.

"It's not Zack," Mackenzie said. "Zack is gone."

"Good," Steph said, matter-of-factly. "He was a waste of space."

There was silence on the line for a moment. It was clear that Steph could have gone the rest of her life without speaking to her sister ever again. It was a fact she had made clear multiple times. They did not hate each other—not by a long shot—but interacting with one another brought up the past. And the past was something that Steph had spent most of her thirty-three years of life running hard from.

As always, Steph sounded half-asleep when she spoke on the phone.

"No sense in getting into details. Bills barely paid. Alcoholic boyfriend with a reputation for throwing right hooks at me. Constant migraines. Which would you like to hear about?"

Mackenzie took a deep breath.

"Well, how about starting with the boyfriend that's beating you?" Mackenzie said. "Why don't you report him for abuse?"

Steph said only laughed. "Too much trouble. No thanks."

Mackenzie bit back a stream of responses to the other things. Among them were: *How about you go back to college, finish working toward your degree, and get out of that dead-end job?* But right now was not the time for such advice. Now, over the phone, things would stay at the surface. They had both learned long ago that it was better that way.

"So spill it," Steph said. "You only ever call when things are going to shit for you. Is it just Zack leaving? Because if it is, let me tell you—that's the best thing that could have happened to you."

"That's part of it," Mackenzie said. "But there's also this case that is getting under my skin in a way that I've never experienced. It's making me feel, I don't know, *inadequate*. Throw in the fact that I invited a married man into bed yesterday and—"

"Did you get lucky?" Steph interrupted.

"God, Steph. That's all you took away from that?"

"It was the only interesting thing I heard. Who was it?"

"An FBI agent that was sent down to help with the case."

"Oh," Steph said, apparently done with the conversation. Silence fell across the line for about five seconds before she repeated the question: "Well, did he?"

"No."

"Ouch," Steph said.

"Do you not feel like talking?" Mackenzie asked.

"Rarely. I mean, we're strangers, Mackenzie. What do you want from me?"

Mackenzie sighed, overcome with sadness.

"I want my sister," Mackenzie said, surprising even herself. "I want a sister that I can call and that will call me from time to time to tell me about the creep at work that has grab-hands."

Steph sighed. It was a sound that seemed to travel the eight hundred miles that separated them and reach out through the phone to slap her in the face.

"That's not me," Steph said. "You know that every time we talk, Dad will come up. And it all goes downhill from there. Even worse, we start talking about Mom."

The word *mom* sent another slap through the phone line. "How is she?" Mackenzie asked.

"The same as always. I talked to her last month. She asked me for some money."

"Did you lend it to her?"

"Mackenzie, I don't have the money *to* lend her."

Another silence filled the phone. Mackenzie had offered to lend Steph money on several occasions but each attempt had been met with scorn, anger, and resentment. So after a while, Mackenzie had simply stopped trying.

"Is that all?" Steph asked.

"One more thing, if you don't mind," Mackenzie said.

"What is it?"

"When you spoke to Mom, did she mention me even once?"

Steph was quiet for a while and then finally answered. When she did, her sleepy voice was back. "You really want to do this to yourself?"

"Did she ask about me?" Mackenzie asked, her voice louder now and more demanding.

"She did. She asked if I thought you would lend her any money. I told her to ask you herself. That was it."

Mackenzie felt overwhelmed with sadness. That was all her mom had ever wanted of her.

She held the phone to her ear, feeling a tear, unsure what to say.

"Look," Steph said. "For real, I have to go."

The phone went dead.

Mackenzie tossed the phone on the bed and stared at it for a moment. The conversation had lasted no more than five minutes but it felt like a lifetime. Still, it had oddly gone much better than their last few phone calls, which had ended with arguments over the family dynamic in regards to who was to blame for their mother's downfall after their father's death. Yet in a way, this call was worse.

She thought about the years that sat like a rotting stretch between the night she found her father dead and the night her mother had been taken to the psychiatric ward of the hospital for the first time. Mackenzie had been seventeen when that had happened; Steph had been in college, working toward a journalism degree. After that, things had gone south for the three of them but Mackenzie was the only one who had managed to endure it all, coming out as on top as possible given the dire circumstances.

She thought of her mother as she finished getting dressed, wondering why the poor woman had chosen to hate her through all of it. It was a question she kept tucked away in the furthest corners of her mind, only bringing it out when she was at her lowest.

Doing everything she could to keep herself from going there, she retrieved her phone, badge, and gun. She then headed out for work, determined. But where did she go from here? What was her next step?

For the first time since being promoted to detective, she felt like she was at a dead end.

Dead end, she thought, the words starting to build an idea in her mind.

She thought about the dirt road the second body had been found alongside. Hadn't it come to a dead end in that field?

And how about the abandoned house? The gravel road that had led to it and the third victim had come to a dead end in a small square of dirt in front the house.

"Dead end," she said out loud as she left her house.

And suddenly, she knew where she had to go.

CHAPTER EIGHTEEN

His living room was mostly dark, illuminated only by the thin shafts of morning sun that managed to creep through the blinds. He sat in an old ragged armchair and looked to the old roll-top desk against the far corner of the room. The cover was rolled up, revealing the items he had kept from each sacrifice.

There was a pocketbook with a wallet inside. Within the wallet, there was a driver's license belonging to Hailey Lizbrook. There was also a skirt that had belonged to the woman he had hung up in the field; a chunk of strawberry blonde hair with black dye at the tips from the woman he had placed behind the abandoned house.

There was still room for reminders he would bring back from the rest of his sacrifices—reminders of each woman he took for the sake of the work the Lord had delegated for him. While he was pleased with how things had gone so far, he knew that there was still work to be done.

He sat in the armchair, staring at his reminders—his *trophies*—and waited for the sun to finish rising. Only when the morning was fully engaged was he to start working again.

Looking at the items on the roll-top desk, he wondered (not for the first time) if he was a bad man. He didn't think so. Someone had to do this work. The hardest jobs were always left to those who did not fear to do them.

But sometimes when he heard the women scream and beg for their lives, he wondered if there was something wrong with him.

When the shafts of lights on the floor went from a translucent yellow to an almost too-bright white, he knew the time had come.

He rose from his chair and walked into the kitchen. From the kitchen, he exited the house through a screen door that led into his backyard.

The yard was small and enclosed by an old chain-link fence that looked both out of place and somehow camouflaged by the neglect of the neighborhood. The grass was tall and overrun with weeds. Bees buzzed and other nameless insects scurried as he approached, making his way through the tall grass.

At the back of the yard, taking up the entire back left corner, was an old shed. It was an eyesore on the already ugly property. He went to it and pulled the door open on its old rusty hinges. It creaked open, revealing the dank darkness inside. Before stepping in, he looked around to the neighboring houses. No one was home. He knew their schedules well.

Now, in the safe light of 9 AM, he stepped into his shed and slid the door closed behind him. The barn was thick with the smell of wood and dust. As he entered, a large rat scurried along the back wall and made its exit through a slot in the boards. He paid the rodent no mind, heading directly to the three long wooden poles that were stacked to the right side of the shed. They were stacked in a miniature pyramid shape, one on top of the other two. Ten days ago, there had been three others there. But those had been put to good use to further his work.

And now, another must be prepared.

He walked to the poles and ran his hand lovingly along the well-worn cedar surface of the one stacked on top. He went to the back of the shed where a small work table was set up. There was an old handsaw, its teeth jagged and rusty, a hammer, and a chisel. He took up the hammer and the chisel and returned to the poles.

He thought of his father as he hefted the hammer. His father had been a carpenter. On many occasions, his father would tell him that the Good Lord Jesus had also been a carpenter. Thinking of his father made him think of his mother. It made him remember why she'd left them when he'd only been seven years old.

He thought of the man that lived up the street and how he would come over when his father was not home. He recalled the squeaking bedsprings and the filthy words that came from the bedroom among his mother's cries—cries that had sounded both happy and hurt all at the same time.

"Out secret," his mother had said. "He's just a friend and your daddy doesn't need to know anything about it, right?"

He'd agreed. Besides, his mother had seemed happy. Which was why he'd been so confused when she left them.

He set his hands on the top pole and closed his eyes. A fly on the wall might have thought that he was praying over the pole or even communicating with it somehow.

When he was done, he opened his eyes and put the hammer and chisel to use.

In the scant light that came in through the cracks in the boards, he started to chisel.

First came N511, then J202.

Next would come a sacrifice.

And he would claim that tonight.

CHAPTER NINETEEN

Mackenzie found herself walking into a small coffee shop with the barest flicker of hope. After she'd made the awkward call to her sister, she'd placed another phone call to someone she hadn't spoken to in quite some time. The conversation had been brief and to the point, concluding in agreeing to meet over coffee.

She looked up now and spotted the man she had called right away. He was hard to miss; in a crowd of rushed people on their way to work, mostly young and well-dressed, his white hair and flannel shirt stood out drastically.

He was turned away from her, and she approached him from behind and placed a gentle hand on his shoulder.

"James," she said. "How are you?"

He turned and smiled widely at her as she sat down in front of him.

"Mackenzie, I swear you just get prettier and prettier," he said.

"And you just get smoother and smoother," she said. "It's good to see you, James."

"Likewise," he said.

James Woerner was pushing seventy but looked closer to eighty. He was tall and skinny, something that had once prompted the officers he once worked with to call him Crane, after Ichabod Crane. It was a name that he'd adapted to himself after he retired from the force and had spent eight years as a consultant for the local PD and, on two occasions, for the state police.

"So what's going on that might be so bad as to have you reach out to an old fart like me?" he asked.

There was humor in the question but Mackenzie felt herself shrinking away from him as she realized that James was the second person in less than two hours to assume that she had called because she was in a spot of trouble.

"I was wondering if you ever had a case that got under your skin," she said. "And I don't mean something that just bothers you. I'm talking about a case that affects you so badly that you get paranoid when you're at home and it feels like every failed lead is your fault."

"I assume you're talking about the poorly named Scarecrow Killer?" James asked.

"How…" she almost asked but then realized she knew the answer, even as James answered it for her.

"I saw your picture in the paper," he said before sipping his coffee. "I was happy for you. You need a case like this under your belt. I seem to remember telling you that you were destined to crack cases like this several years ago."

"You did," she said.

"Yet you're still hanging out in the trenches with the local PD?"

"I am."

"Is Nelson treating you okay?"

"As well as he can, given the crew he has working for him. He's all but put me at the front of this case. I'm hoping it's a way for him to let me prove myself so all of the macho bullshit from the others can come to an end."

"Still working with Porter?"

"I was, but he was reassigned when an FBI agent showed up."

"Working with the feds," James said with a smile. "I believe that was another prediction I made about you. But I digress."

He smiled and leaned forward.

"Tell me about why this case is affecting you so badly. And if you keep it at a surface level, I'll take my coffee and leave. I have a busy day of doing absolutely nothing ahead of me."

She smiled.

"The glamorous retired lifestyle," she said.

"You're damned right," James said. "But don't try to sidestep."

She knew better than to dance around a direct request. She'd learned that when he had taken her under his wing five years ago, teaching her the basics of profiling and how to get into the mind of a criminal. The man was stubborn as hell and always got right to the point—which, Mackenzie always thought, was why they had gotten along so well.

"I think it's because it's a man that seems to be killing *only* women. More than that, he's killing women that use their bodies to make a living."

"And that bothers you why?"

It stung her heart to say it, but she got it out anyway.

"It makes me think of my sister. And when I think of my sister, I think of my father. And when I go there, I feel like a failure because I haven't caught this guy yet."

"Your sister was a stripper?" James asked.

She nodded.

"For about six months. She hated it. But the money was good enough to help her get on her feet after a rough patch. It always made me sad to think of her doing that for a living. And while I don't see my sister on those wooden poles when I visit the sites, I know that the chances are good that the women this guy is killing probably had lives very similar to Steph."

"Now, Mackenzie, you do know that always going back to your father when things aren't going your way on a case is self-abuse, right? There's no need to torment yourself over that."

"I know. But I can't help it."

"Well, let's look away from that for now. I assume you called me for guidance of some sort, right?"

"Yes."

"Well, the bad news is that everything I have read in the news is dead-on to what I would say. You're looking for a man with an aversion to sex that has likely had issues with a wife, sister, or mother in his life. I'd also add, though, that this guy doesn't get out much. His inclination to display his victims in such rural areas makes me think he's a small-town boy. He probably lives in a ramshackle part of town. If not *this* town, then certainly nowhere outside of a one-hundred-mile radius or so. But that's just a guess."

"So we could narrow our search for someone that has cedar poles at the ready in the seedier parts of town?"

"For a start. Now, tell me, are there any details you have noticed about the scenes that might have taken the back seat to the overarching horridness of the scenes themselves?"

"Just the numbers," she said.

"Yes, I read about them, but only twice. The media is too obsessed with the profession of the women to dwell on something they don't understand right away. Like those numbers. But remember: never take a crime scene for granted. Every scene has a story to tell. Even if that story is hidden in something that is seemingly trivial at first, there's a story. It's your job to find it, read it, and figure out what it means."

She pondered that. What, she wondered, had she overlooked?

"There's something else I need to ask you," she said. "I'm about to do something I've never done before and I don't want it to make my situation worse. It could potentially get deeper under my skin."

James eyed her for a moment and gave her the same sly smile that had sometimes creeped her out when he had served as her mentor. It meant he had figured something out without being told and he now held that over her.

"You're going back to the murder scenes," he said.

"Yes."

"You're going to try to enter the mind of the killer," he said. "You're going to try to see the scenes as a man with some flaw inside of him—with a hatred of women and a deranged sort of fear towards sex."

"That's the plan," she said.

"And when are you doing this?"

"As soon as I leave here."

James seemed to consider this for a moment. He took another sip from his coffee and nodded his approval.

"I know you're fully capable of it," he said. "But are you mentally *ready*?"

Mackenzie shrugged and said, "I have to be."

"That can be dangerous," he warned. "If you start seeing the scenes through the eyes of the killer, it can also distort the way you've been trained to see those sorts of scenes. You need to be ready for that—to draw the line between that sort of dark inspiration and your ultimate need to find this guy and take him down."

"I know," Mackenzie said softly.

James drummed his fingers along the sides of his cup. "Would you like for me to come with you?"

"I thought about asking you," she said. "But I think this is something I'm going to have to do by myself."

"That's probably the right decision," James said. "I must warn you, though: as you try to see things from a killer's point of view, never allow yourself to jump to conclusions. Try to start fresh. Don't close your mind off with assumptions like, this guy just hates women. Let the scene talk to you before you project yourself towards the scene."

Mackenzie grinned in spite of herself. "That sounds pretty New Age," she said. "Have you turned a new leaf?"

"No. The leaves stop turning after retirement. Now, how much longer do you have before you set out on this little quest?"

"Soon," she said. "I'd like to visit the first one by noon."

"Good," he said. "That means you have some time. So, for the time being, push this Scarecrow Killer crap to the side. Go order yourself a coffee and entertain an old man for a while. What do you say?"

She gave him a look that she had tried so hard to keep from him for the year or so he'd mentored her. It was the look of a young girl looking to her father with a need to please and make him happy. While she had never psychoanalyzed herself to uncover this truth, she had known it right away, from the first week she'd spent two hours of two days with him. James Woerner had been a father figure to her during that time in her life and it was something for which she would be forever grateful.

So when he asked her to grab a cup of coffee and keep him company, she happily obliged. The cornfield, the gravel roads, and that old abandoned house had been sitting for ages, unmoving. They could wait another hour or so.

CHAPTER TWENTY

Under James Woerner's brief tutelage, one of the things he had praised her for over and over again was her instinct. She had a gut, he had said, that was better than reading palms or tea leaves for an indication of what to do next. That's why she wasted no time with the cornfield where Hailey Lizbrook's body had been discovered or the open field where the second body had been strung up.

She went directly back to the abandoned house where the latest victim had been displayed. During her first visit, she'd felt as if the darkened windows had been a set of eyes, watching her every move. She had known it deep in her heart then and there that the scene had more to offer. But after everything that had happened with Ellis Pope, it had been an inclination that she had not been able to investigate.

She parked her car in front of the place and stared at the house through the windshield for a moment before getting out. From the front, the house looked just as foreboding, like the model for every haunted house that had ever been committed to page or film. She looked at the house, trying to see it the same way a murderer would see it. Why choose this location? Was it the house itself or the overwhelming sense of isolation that had appealed to him?

This, in turn, made her wonder how long the killer had scoped out the sites for where he would display his victims. The coroner's reports seemed to indicate that the bodies were brought to these sites and killed—not killed beforehand and simply put up for viewing at the display sites. Why? What was the point?

Mackenzie finally got out of the car. Before walking toward the dilapidated porch, she walked around the side of the house and to the place where the third victim had been strung up. The body and the pole had been removed; the area was visibly unsettled, trampled by the foot traffic of the handful of authorities that had visited the site. Mackenzie stood where the pole had been, the hole still visible and the loose dirt perfectly outlining it.

She hunkered down and placed her hand on the hole. She looked to the surrounding forest and the back of the house, trying to see what the killer had seen in the moment he had started to assault the woman. A chill traced her spine as she closed her eyes and tried to envision it.

The whip he was using had multiple lashes at the end, potentially barbed, gauging from the wound patterns. Even still, it had to be used with great force to open up the flesh the way it did.

He would probably stalk the victims first, walking circles around the pole, enjoying their cries and their pleading. Then something happens. Something clicks in his head or maybe the victim says something that triggers him. That's when he starts whipping them.

Here, at this location, he had attacked with more fury than before; the lashes weren't contained just to the back as they had been before, but reached to the chest and stomach, a few even slicing into her lower buttocks. At some point, the killer thinks his work is done and stops. And then what? Does he make sure they are dead before he leaves the site in a truck or a van? How long does he stay here with them?

If he's killing for more than just pleasure but out of some aversion to women and/or sex, then he probably hangs out for a while, watching them bleed, watching the life slip out of their eyes. As they die, maybe he is then brave enough to look at their bodies, to cup a breast experimentally with a trembling hand. Does he feel safe or powerful, disgusted or elated to see them bleed, to watch the cloak of death fall over them, leaving their bare bodies on display?

Mackenzie opened her eyes and looked to the hole that her hand still rested on. The reports showed that all three holes had been dug crudely with a shovel, at a rapid pace rather than with much cleaner and more accurate post-hole diggers. He'd been in a hurry to get things started and then he'd placed the poles in each hole and packed the dirt back in. Where had the women been then? Drugged? Unconscious?

Mackenzie stood up and walked back to the front of the house. While she had no real reason to believe the killer had been inside, the fact that he had selected the yard outside as one of his trophy stands made the house guilty by association.

She stepped up onto the porch and it creaked under her weight right away. In fact, the entire porch seemed to settle around her weight. Somewhere out in the forest, a bird called out in response.

She made her way inside the house, pushing past a mostly deteriorated wooden door that scuffed against the floor. She was instantly assaulted by the smell of dust and mildew, the overall scent of neglect.

Stepping into the house was like stepping into a black-and-white movie. Once inside, that old gut instinct that James had once held in such a high regard told her there was nothing abnormal here, no huge *a-ha* sort of clue that would bring this case to a close.

Still, she couldn't resist. She explored the empty rooms and hallways. She observed the cracked walls and peeling plaster, trying to imagine a family once living in this ruined space. Eventually, she made her way to the back of the house where it looked like a kitchen had once thrived. Old cracked linoleum clung to the floor in curling sheets, revealing a rotten floor beneath. She looked across the kitchen and saw the two windows that looked to the backyard— the same two windows that she'd felt were staring at her on her first time out here.

She walked across the kitchen, sticking beside the neglected counter along the far wall in order to avoid the questionable floor. As she moved, she realized how utterly quiet it was in the house. This was a place for ghosts and memories, not a desperate detective reaching blindly for some sense of what a killer was going through. Regardless, she made her way to the rear wall and looked out of the first window, sitting to the left of an old battered kitchen sink.

The location of where the pole and the third victim had been was visible from the window without obstruction. From inside the house, it did not look nearly as intimidating. Mackenzie tried to envision the order of things from her place at the window, as if looking at the imagined scene through a TV. She saw the killer bringing the woman to the pole that he had already placed there. She wondered if she was unconscious or somehow inebriated, wobbling on her feet with his hands under her arms or at her back.

That spurred a thought that no one had bothered checking yet. *How does he get them to the pole? Are they knocked out? Drugged? Does he simply overpower them? Maybe we should get the coroner to check for any substance that causes lethargic behavior...*

She stared at the scene for a bit longer, starting to feel the seclusion of the forest along the backyard pressing in on her. There was nothing out there, only trees, hidden animals, and just the slightest stirring of wind.

She exited the kitchen and made her way back out into what had once been a living room. An old scarred desk sat against the wall. It was visibly warped along the top and many of the scattered papers on it looked like leaves that had been cast to the ground and rained on for years. Mackenzie made her way over to the desk and rummaged through the few papers.

She saw invoices for pig feed and grain. The oldest was dated June of 1977 and came from a farm supply in Chinook, Nebraska. Notebook paper that had been aged so badly that its blue lines were missing held someone's faded handwriting. Mackenzie glanced over the writing and saw what looked to be notes for a Sunday school lesson. She saw references to Noah and the flood, David and Goliath, and Samson. Under the mess of paper were two books: a devotional called *God's Healing Word* and a Bible that looked so old that she feared it would crumble into dust at her touch.

Still, she found that she was unable to look away from the Bible. Seeing it brought to mind visions of the crucifixion that she had learned about during the handful of times she had ventured into a church with her mother at an early age. She thought of Christ on the cross and what it had represented, and found herself reaching for the book.

She thought of the cross Christ had died on and superimposed that sight with the sight of those three women on their poles. They had ruled out religious motive but she couldn't help but wonder.

She opened the Bible and flipped past the front matter, heading directly for the table of contents. She knew very little about the Bible, so half of the names of the books were not familiar to her.

She scanned the table of contents absentmindedly, about to put it down, when suddenly she spotted something and her heart started beating faster. The names of the books. The numbers beside them.

As she saw the abbreviations, it reminded her of something else.

The pole.

The numbers.

N511

J202

With trembling hands, she started at the top of the Contents page, placing her finger on *Genesis*. She then scrolled down with her finger, looking for a book that began with "N."

Within seconds, she stopped at the listing for the book of Numbers.

She flipped through the dusty pages, the smell of rot wafting into her face. She located Numbers and then scanned through for Chapter 5. When she found that, she then ran her finger along the page until she came to verse 11.

N511. Numbers, Chapter 5, verse 11.

She read, and with each word, her heart beat faster. It felt as if the temperature of the house had dropped by about twenty degrees.

And the LORD spoke unto Moses, saying, Speak unto the children of Israel, and say unto them, If any man's wife go aside, and commit a trespass against him, and a man lie with her carnally, and it be hid from the eyes of her husband, and be kept close, and she be defiled, and there be no witness against her, neither she be taken with the manner; and the spirit of jealousy come upon him, and he be jealous of his wife, and she be defiled: or if the spirit of

jealousy come upon him, and he be jealous of his wife, and she be
not defiled: Then shall the man bring his wife unto the priest…

She read it several times, hands shaking, feeling excited and sick at the same time. The passage filled her with a sense of foreboding that made her stomach a little queasy.

She flipped back to the table of contents. She saw that there were several books that began with J, but solving that little riddle wasn't her specialty. Besides, she was pretty sure she had enough to go on with the passage from Numbers.

Mackenzie closed the Bible and placed it back with the forgotten papers. She ran out of the house and back to her car, suddenly in a hurry.

She needed to get back to the station.

More than that, she needed to speak with a pastor.

This killer was not as random as everyone thought.

He had an MO.

And she was about to crack it.

CHAPTER TWENTY ONE

Mackenzie had not stepped foot into a church since the wedding of her college roommate. After her father died, her mother had tried dragging her and Steph to church on numerous occasions and it was for that very reason that Mackenzie did everything she could to avoid it.

Still, as she entered the sanctuary of New Life Methodist Church, she had to admit that there was a certain degree of beauty here. It was more than the stained glass windows and the ornate altar—there was something else entirely that, quite frankly, she could not put her finger on.

As she neared the front of the sanctuary, she saw an older man sitting in one of the pews to the front. He had apparently not heard her enter because he had his head down, reading in a book.

"Pastor Simms?" she asked. Her voice boomed like the Almighty in the cavernous sanctuary.

The man looked up from his book and turned to face her. He was a man in his fifties, dressed in a button-down shirt and khakis. He wore the sort of eyeglasses that instantly made him appear to be infinitely kind.

"Detective White, I presume?" he asked, getting to his feet.

"You presumed correctly," she said.

He looked a bit shocked but met her at the head of the sanctuary all the same.

"Forgive my surprise," he said. "When your Chief Nelson called to request some of my time for your research, I wasn't expecting a woman. Due to the heinous nature of the crimes, I find it rather odd that a woman would be heading it up. No offense to you, of course."

"None taken."

"You know, Clark speaks favorably of you."

The name *Clark* threw her off and it took her a moment to realize that he was talking about Nelson—Police Chief Clark Nelson.

"I've heard that a lot lately," she said.

"Well then, that must be nice."

"And unexpected," she said.

Simms nodded, as if he understood perfectly. "Nelson's a bit of a blowhard at times. But he's also extremely kind when he needs to be. I imagine that's a hard part of himself to show at work."

"So he attends this church?" Mackenzie asked.

"Oh yes," he said. "Every Sunday. But I digress. Please," he added, gesturing to the pew he had been sitting on. "Have a seat."

Mackenzie did so and looked to the book Pastor Simms had been reading from and was not at all surprised to find that it was a Bible.

"So, Chief Nelson tells me that you have questions about scripture that may be able to lead to the arrest of the man that has been killing these poor women."

She pulled out her cell phone and pulled up the picture she had snapped of the old Bible from the abandoned house. She handed it to him and he took it, adjusting his glasses as he looked at it.

"Numbers, chapter five, verses eleven to twenty or so. Do you think you could tell me how you interpret the verse?" she asked.

He glanced at the picture briefly and then handed the phone back.

"Well, it's pretty self-explanatory. Not all Biblical passages need to be decoded. This one simply speaks of adulterous women being forced to drink bitter waters. If they were pure, no harm would come to them. But if they had engaged in sexual relations with anyone other than their husbands, the waters would bring a curse upon them."

She pondered that.

"The killer has carved N511 on each post he has hung a victim from," she said. "And based on the sort of women he has been choosing, the allegory seems pretty fitting."

"Yes, I'd agree," Simms said.

"He's also carving J202 into the posts. There are too many books of the Bible that begin with *J* for me to make an educated guess. I was hoping you'd have some insight?"

"Well, Numbers is an Old Testament book and if this killer is killing based on what he thinks is Old Testament law—however misguided his interpretations and actions may be—I think it's safe to say that this other reference would be Old Testament as well. If that's the case, I feel certain that it's referring to the book of Joshua. In Chapter Twenty of Joshua, God speaks of Cities of Refuge. These were cities where people who had accidentally killed others could flee to without prosecution."

Mackenzie chewed on this for a moment, her heart racing, something starting to click inside. She picked up the Bible and found Joshua and dug up the passage. When she found it, she read it out loud, a bit creeped out by the sound of scripture coming out of her voice in this empty church.

Then the Lord said to Joshua: Tell the Israelites to designate the cities of refuge, as I instructed you through Moses, so that anyone who kills a person accidentally and unintentionally may flee there and find protection from the avenger of blood. When they flee to one of these cities, they are to stand in the entrance of the city gate and state their case before the elders of that city. Then the elders are to admit the fugitive into their city and provide a place to live among them. If the avenger of blood comes in pursuit...

She trailed off here, astounded, knowing she had finally figured out the source of the numbers. It was both thrilling and deflating. She had a window into his MO now—and yet it was still so vague. None of this could bring her to his front door.

"There's more, you know," Simms said.

"Yes, I see that," she said. "But I think that's enough. Tell me, Pastor, do you know how many of these Cities of Refuge there were?"

"Six in all," Simms said.

"Do you know where they were located?"

"Roughly," he replied.

He picked up the Bible and turned to the back, showing her a series of glossaries and maps. He came to a map that represented Israel in biblical times and, adjusting his glasses again, pointed out six locations.

"Of course," he said, "these locations may not be exact, but—"

Her heart started beating hard as she made a connection that almost seemed too good to be true. She gripped the book tightly.

"May I take a picture?" she asked.

"Of course," he replied.

She photographed it with shaking hands.

"Detective, what is it?" he asked, studying her. "Have I been of help in some way I don't understand?"

"More than you know," she said.

CHAPTER TWENTY TWO

When Mackenzie entered the conference room, the place was abuzz. Nancy sat at her usual spot at the end of the table, divvying out the most updated reports on the Scarecrow Killer case. Policemen were taking their seats at the table, murmuring solemnly as if they were attending a funeral. As Mackenzie wedged her way to the front of the room where she saw Nelson speaking to another officer, she noticed that she was getting a lot of looks from the officers she passed. Some were still scowling at her as they had three days before in this very same room. But (and maybe this was her imagination) some were looking at her with genuine interest and, dare she say it, respect.

Nelson saw her coming and ended his conversation with the other officer right away. He put an arm around her and turned her away from the crowd that still continued to gather in the room. "This news," he said. "Is it going to net us an arrest within the next few hours?"

"I don't know," Mackenzie said. "But it can certainly narrow our search. It's going to bring us very close."

"Then you run this show," he said. "Can you do that?"

"Yes," she said, ignoring the pit of worry that bubbled up in her stomach.

"Well then, here we go," he said. With that, he turned to face the room and slapped his meaty hands down on the table several times. "Okay, everybody," he shouted. "Take a seat and zip your mouths," he said. "Mackenzie has a break in the case and you'll give her your full attention. Save any questions until she's done."

To Mackenzie's surprise, Nelson took one of the remaining chairs against the wall, pushed away from the large conference table. He looked to her and that was when she realized that it was all on her. Maybe it was a test or maybe Nelson was just at the end of his rope. Either way, this was her chance to grab this precinct by the balls and prove her worth.

She looked out to the room and saw Porter sitting among the faces. He gave her a quick smile, almost like he wanted to ensure no one else saw it. It was probably the sweetest thing he'd ever done for her and she found that Porter was starting to surprise her at every turn.

"I revisited one of the crime scenes this morning," Mackenzie explained. "While the visit itself did not reveal the break, it led me straight to it. As many of you know, each post the killer has strapped the women to has had two code-like groupings of letters and numbers: N511 and J202. After speaking with a pastor earlier today, I discovered that these are references to Numbers 5:11 and Joshua 20:2.

"The Numbers passage talks about an Old Testament approach to adultery. Any adulterous woman was brought to the priests and given what were called bitter waters. The thought was that the blessed water would curse adulterous women and would not affect a pure woman. In essence, it was the church's way of judging or accusing women thought to be unclean.

"As for the reference to Joshua, that passage refers to Cities of Refuge—cities that men could escape to if they had accidentally committed murder or killed to protect themselves, their families, or their people. In these Cities of Refuge, the murdered could not be prosecuted. In fact, it is said in the passage that all men residing in a City of Refuge would be spared from the avenger of blood.

"Now, according to the pastor I spoke with, there were six of the cities. And that leads me to believe that there are going to be at least three more murders."

"Why is that?" Nelson asked, disregarding his earlier rule of keeping all questions for the end.

"I believe the killer is killing these women to use them as a representation of each City of Refuge. And, as he is killing them, he believes he is taking on the role of the avenger of blood. More than that, he is, in a sense, building a city."

The room fell silent for a moment as they waited for her to explain. She turned to the wall behind her where a well-used whiteboard had recently been cleaned. She grabbed a marker and drew a crude map from memory, sketching out the map Pastor Simms had showed her in the church.

"These are the rough locations of the six cities," she said, placing large dots along her crude map. They made a crude oval shape, each city almost the same distance from one another.

"Now, if you were to take a map of the area containing the sites where we have found each of the bodies," she said, "it would resemble this almost exactly."

Right away, Nancy started typing something into her computer at the back of the table. Without looking up from her screen, she said, "I'll bring up a map," she said. "Lights, please."

The officer closest to the light switch hit the lights while another flipped on the projector that sat in the middle of the cluttered conference table. Mackenzie stepped to the side to allow the light to shine directly on the dry erase board.

Nancy had brought up the same map that was attached to the reports that she had handed out earlier. It showed each highway, secondary road, and town within a one-hundred-fifty-mile radius. On the map, three Xs had been placed where each of the victims had been found.

"While the locations don't line up perfectly," Mackenzie said, "they are extremely close in proximity. What this means is that if this isn't simply a coincidence—and at this point, I think it's clear that it is *not*—then we can pinpoint the rough location of where the next crime scene might be."

"How do we know which order he'll go in?" one of the officers at the table asked. "If there are three remaining, is there any guarantee he's going on geographical order?"

"No, there's no guarantee," Mackenzie admitted. "But so far, that's been the case."

"And are we still unsure about *how* he's selecting the victims?" Porter asked.

"That's being checked as we speak," Mackenzie said. "We have men checking in with the three strip clubs in that hundred-mile radius. But I think we also need to assume that he wouldn't look beyond prostitutes as well."

"What about these *bitter waters*?" someone else asked. "What kind of water is that?"

"I don't know for sure," Mackenzie said. "But we've already informed the coroner to check the stomach contents of the victims to see if there is anything out of the ordinary: poisons, chemicals, anything like that. I personally believe that it could just be holy water and if that's the case, it will be impossible to pinpoint it."

"You mean blessed water doesn't glow magically?" another officer asked. There were a few chuckles around the table.

"Hey," Nelson said, taking the front of the room again. He went to the board and grabbed a red marker. He circled the phantom area on the projected map that seemed to align the best with the fourth city on the map Mackenzie had drawn.

"I'm putting White in charge of locking down this area right here," he said. "I want at least eight available men out there within the next hour to take a survey of the place. Get a lay of the land, learn the roads, and stay on patrol within the area until you hear otherwise from me. Nancy, I need you to get on the phone with the State PD and request the use of a helicopter to sweep the area."

"Yes, sir," Nancy said.

"Another thing," Mackenzie said. "Unmarked cars only. The last thing we want is to tip this guy off."

Nelson considered this and she could tell something about it irritated him. "Well, with only four unmarked cars, that limits us. So I'm allowing patrol cars, but not to be parked or stationary. Now, with everything we now know, there's no excuse to not catch this guy before a fourth woman has to die. Any questions?"

No one said anything as everyone within the room got to their feet. There was a tingle of excitement in the air that Mackenzie could almost feel like a physical presence. Officers started to file out eagerly, sensing that the end of this wretched case was upon them. She knew the mentality; at this point, anyone could potentially have the chance to arrest the suspect. Although someone else (in this case, her) had made the connections and presented them with an endgame solution, it was anybody's ballgame now.

As Mackenzie headed for the door, Nelson stopped her. "That's some damn fine work, Mackenzie. And I'll tell you something else, too: Ellington was singing your praises when he got back to Quantico. I got a call from his director and they were complimenting you."

"Thanks."

"Now if I could just keep you from chasing down overweight online journalists and scaring the hell out of them, I think you'd have a promising career ahead of you. That Pope creep has had two different lawyers calling after you. I don't think he's going to leave this alone."

"Sorry, Chief," she said, meaning it.

"Well, push that to the back burner," Nelson said. "For now, let's concentrate on catching this killer. Journalists are almost as bad but at least Ellis Pope isn't stringing women up by poles and beating them to death."

She cringed internally at how lightheartedly Nelson was referring to the victims. It reminded her that, even in the midst of a sudden and unexpected stream of confidence and praise from the man, he was the same creature of habit he had been when she had first started working under him.

"And if it's okay with you," he said, "I'm driving up with you. If I've put you in charge of this scene, I'd like to be your wingman."

"Sure," she said, instantly hating the idea.

As they walked out of the conference room, she looked around for Porter. It was funny in an ironic sort of way how much she'd prefer to share a car with Porter as this case drew to a close. Maybe it was familiarity or just the fact that she still felt like Nelson was a little too much of a chauvinist to take her seriously, despite praises from the FBI.

But Porter had gotten lost in the shuffle and excitement as everyone had filed out of the conference room. She did not see him in the hallway as she stopped by her office to retrieve her badge and gun and he was nowhere to be found in the parking lot.

Nelson met her at the car and it wasn't even a question of who would drive. He instantly got behind the wheel and seemed very impatient as he waited for her to get into the passenger seat and buckle her seat belt. She did her best to hide her irritation but thought it really didn't matter. Nelson was so caught up in the prospect of catching the Scarecrow Killer that she was basically an afterthought—just the cog in the mostly man-driven machine that had brought them this far.

Suddenly, Ellington's suggestion of trying to get into the FBI seemed more appealing than ever.

"Ready to catch this asshole?" Nelson asked as they pulled out of the parking lot behind two patrol cars.

Mackenzie bit at her bottom lip to hide the sarcastic smile that tried to spread there and said:

"More than you know."

CHAPTER TWENTY THREE

Mackenzie's phone started ringing less than ten minutes into her ride with Nelson. She checked the number on the display and although she had not yet saved it, it was fresh and familiar in her mind. She had nearly forgotten that Ellington had sent a text stating that he would call her. She knew he'd sent the text that morning but it seemed like a very long time ago. She checked the time on her phone's task bar and saw that it was only 3:16. This day was turning out to be incredibly long.

She ignored the call, not wanting to add another level of complexity to what was turning out to be an already chaotic afternoon. At the same time she was ignoring Ellington's call, Nelson was on the phone with Nancy. He spoke curtly, straight and to the point. It was clear that he was on edge and beyond stressed out, something that Mackenzie was beginning to feel herself.

He ended the call several seconds later and started nervously tapping at the steering wheel with his thumbs. "Nancy just spoke to the State boys," he said. "They'll have a helicopter flying over the area within an hour and a half."

"That's good news," Mackenzie said.

"Tell me," Nelson said. "Do you think he's killing the women before he puts them on the poles or does he kill them there?"

"There's nothing solid to prove either way," Mackenzie said. "However, the first scene in the cornfield makes me think the women are alive when he puts them on the poles. There were marks on the ground where the whip or whatever he uses was dragged."

"So?"

"So, he was pacing. He was anxious and biding his time. If the woman was already dead, why wait around with the whip?"

Nelson nodded and gave her a smile of appreciation. "We're going to nail this bastard," he said, still drumming on the steering wheel.

Mackenzie badly wanted to join in on his enthusiasm, but something felt incomplete. She almost felt as if she had overlooked something but could not for the life of her figure out what it was. She remained quiet, pondering this silently, as Nelson drove on.

They entered what Nelson was referring to as the Area of Interest twenty minutes later. She had listened to several brief phone calls from Nelson's end during the drive and gathered that Nelson was setting up a perimeter of sorts to block in an area of thirty square miles. The area consisted of mostly scrub land and secondary roads. A few of those secondary roads were surrounded by cornfields just like the site of the original crime scene that had started all of this madness.

As Nelson drove them down such a road, the BC radio squawked at them. "Detective White, are you out there?" a man's voice asked.

Mackenzie looked to Nelson, as if for approval. He gestured to the CD radio installed under the dash with a smile. "Go ahead," he said. "It's your show."

Mackenzie unclasped the mic from the radio and clicked down the send button. "This is White. What have you got?"

"I'm out here off of State Route 411 and came across a side road—nothing more than an old gravel road, really. The road heads straight into a cornfield and is not on the maps. It's about half a mile long and dead ends into a small clearing in the cornfield."

"Okay," she said. "Did you find something?"

"That's putting it lightly, Detective," the officer on the other end said. "I think you need to get out here as fast as you can."

*

It was beyond eerie to find herself standing in another cornfield. It was almost like she had come full circle, only it did not feel like she was coming to the end of something. Quite the contrary, it felt like she was starting all over.

She stood at the edge of the clearing with Nelson and Officer Lent, the man that had contacted her on the radio. The three of them stood among the thinned cornstalks and looked out to the small clearing.

A wooden pole had been erected in the middle of the clearing. Unlike the other poles they had recently seen that were identical to this one, there was no body strung up on it. The pole was bare and looked almost like some weird sort of ancient monolith in the empty clearing.

Slowly, Mackenzie walked up to it. It was cedar, the same as the other three. She got down to her knees and felt the earth around the bottom of the pole. It was soft and had very obviously been loosened and then packed back down rather recently.

"This pole hasn't been here very long," Mackenzie said. "The loose dirt is very fresh. I'd almost guess it was done earlier today."

"So he preps the sites before he brings his victims," Nelson speculated. "I don't know if that's genius or cocky."

While Mackenzie was repulsed by the word *genius* being tied to the killer in any way, she ignored him. She went to the back of the pole and instantly spied the etchings along the bottom, several inches from the loose dirt that held the pole into the ground: N511/J202.

"I wouldn't say it's either," Mackenzie said. "What I do know is that he's essentially left us his business card. We know he's coming back, and he'll probably have his latest victim with him."

As she got back to her feet, she was struck by a sense of vengeance that she had never felt before. The man behind these crimes had somehow shaken her. He had become a specter of sorts, a ghost with the ability to haunt her house, her mind, and her confidence. He had her jumping at the sound of creaking floorboards and getting to such a low point that she was hitting on larger-than-life FBI agents. He'd affected her so much that she hadn't had the energy or emotion to care that Zack had finally left.

On top of that, he was taking women as his victims simply because they used their bodies as a means to make a living. And who the hell was he to judge them for that?

"I want to be here," Mackenzie said. "I want to be on patrol or stakeout or whatever we do to make sure we catch him. I want to put the cuffs on the fucker."

She knew it sounded selfish, but she didn't care. In that moment, she didn't give a damn what Nelson thought of her. She didn't care if he went back to the boys at the station and laughed about how the cute little woman had demanded things from him. Suddenly, catching the man behind these murders was more important than anything—including her job and her reputation.

"I can see to that," Nelson said with a smile. "Good to see a pissed off spark in you, White. I didn't know you had it in you."

She bit back the remark that danced on her tongue, simply thinking it instead.

Neither did I.

CHAPTER TWENTY FOUR

Mackenzie felt positive that the killer would not strike until night, and the others agreed with her. That gave them all four more hours of daylight to get ready for what they hoped would be a successful bust. Even if something *did* happen before nightfall, there were three patrol cars stationed along State Route 411, keeping an eye out for a vehicle entering the dirt road that led to the site the killer had prepared. With the addition of a State PD helicopter on the way to assist, it felt like a victory even before the sun was down.

Mackenzie was in one of the unmarked cars along State Route 411, relieved to be by herself. Nelson had busied himself with heading back to the station to meet with an advisor from the State PD, allowing her to stay behind and keep her eyes on the scene and retain control of the case. Her car was parked a mile and a quarter away from the dirt road, partially hidden from 411 by having pulled backwards into the entrance to what had once been an old cutaway road farmers had used to get from one cornfield to the other.

She'd been sitting there for fifteen minutes and the only car she'd seen go by was a police car, leaving the site and heading back to the station. She still felt certain that there would be no activity until well into the night and knew that she had a long stretch of waiting ahead of her. She wondered if Nelson had given her this duty to keep her out of his hair or if he saw it as giving her a position that kept her front and center of events as they unfolded.

With a sigh and a glance out to the uneventful stretch of State Route 411, Mackenzie picked up her phone and stared at the missed call notification from where Ellington had tried calling her an hour and a half ago. She did her best not to recall the events of yesterday evening when she had made an ass of herself in his presence as she pressed the notification bar. When his number came up, she pressed it right away before she had time to change her mind.

He answered on the third ring and when he did, she hated that it was so good to hear his voice. "Ellington here," he said.

"It's Mackenzie White," she said. "I was returning your call."

"Oh, hey! I hear you guys have a promising break."

"Seems like it, but time will tell. We found the next pole, already set up and ready to go."

"I heard. How do you feel about that?"

"Good," she said.

"You sound doubtful."

"It just seems too good to be true. I feel like there's something missing."

"Maybe there is," Ellington said. "Your instincts are pretty sharp. I wouldn't question them."

"I usually don't."

An awkward silence fell between them and Mackenzie found herself digging for something new to talk about. He'd already heard about the break in the case, so it was useless to rehash it all. *This is pathetic, Mackenzie,* she thought.

"So," Ellington said, breaking the silence. "I took the liberty of working up a profile after I got word about the religious ties. The chances are very good that we're looking for someone with religion in his background. Maybe even a priest or pastor, although history points to an upbringing in a strict religious home. Maybe he went to a private religious school. I'm also thinking he either had no mother at home *or* a mother that got around. He probably acted out as a kid—not in the extreme ways we're seeing right now, but more basic kid-trouble."

"What's all this based on?" she asked. "Just past cases?"

"Yeah, mostly," he said. "I can't take the credit for these insights at all. But truth be told, it's a formula that works about seventy percent of the time."

"Okay, so if this site doesn't pan out, we keep an eye out for one of about one thousand possible suspects."

"Maybe not so many. Based on my profile, I also assume this guy is a local. If he's mapping out his own city, as you have pointed out, I'd say he grew up around there. And because of that, I made a few calls. There's a Catholic grade school within sixty miles of Omaha. There's one more in the state, but I'm betting the one closest to Omaha is going to be your best bet."

"That's amazing," Mackenzie said.

"What is?"

"Just like that, you've narrowed down the search and even have a potential source of background information."

"Well, the *I* in FBI *does* stand for investigation." He laughed a bit at his own joke but when Mackenzie did not, he shut it down.

"Thanks, Ellington."

"Sure. One last thing before you go, though."

"What's that?" she asked, nervous, hoping he wouldn't bring up her embarrassing advances of the night before.

"When I gave my report to my director, I told him you were amazing and that I tried to sway you to the dark side."

She felt flattered.

"The dark side being the Bureau?"

"Right. Anyway, he seemed interested. So if you ever do get that itch to head out our way, I can give you his contact information. It might be a conversation worth having."

She thought this over and while she wanted to say more, to tell him how much she appreciated him, she only managed a simple "Thanks" in response. The very idea seemed too dreamlike. Great things like that tended not to happen to her.

"You okay over there?" Ellington asked.

"Yeah, I'm fine. I need to go, though. This thing is wrapping up down here and I need to stay focused."

"I hear that. Go get 'em."

She grinned in spite of herself. While he may have been a larger-than-life figure to her, Ellington was also proving that he was just as cheesy and flawed as everyone else.

She killed the call and looked out to State Route 411 again. She started to feel antsy, like she was wasting her time by simply sitting there. She pulled up the web browser on her phone and typed in a search for local Catholic grade schools, and found that Ellington had been spot on with his findings.

She saved the address to her phone and then pulled up Nelson's number. He answered after the fourth ring and sounded pissed to have been disrupted from brown-nosing the State guys.

"What's up, White?"

"I want to check on a lead, sir," she said. "It will require me to leave 411 for two or three hours, though."

"Absolutely not," Nelson said. "You're leading this thing, so you have to stay around. This is your show, White. Don't even *think* about letting it get away from you. If we haven't got this guy by tomorrow, we'll talk again. If it's a really promising lead, I can send someone else to check it out."

"No," Mackenzie said. "It's just a hunch."

"Okay," he said. "Keep put until I say otherwise."

She couldn't even reply before he hung up.

With that, she pulled up the address of the Catholic school on her GPS and saved it. She then looked to the right where, a bit further down State Route 411, a lone pole remained empty in a cornfield, awaiting a sacrifice.

She knew she should stay put, should follow orders and sit here for four hours doing nothing.

But as she sat there, something gnawed away at her. What if he killed the victims *before* he brought them out?

If so, that meant there was a girl trapped somewhere, right now, being tortured, a girl who would die while Mackenzie merely sat there and waited for her dead body to show up.

She couldn't stand the thought of it.

And what if that Catholic school—the only one in the area, the one that fit the FBI's profile perfectly—could give her a name? An ID?

That could bring them to the killer before he arrived her. It could perhaps save the next victim before it was too late.

Mackenzie sat there, waiting, burning up inside as she could hear the next victim's screams in her head. Each passing minute was agony.

Finally, she floored the gas and peeled out of there.

She pulled up Holy Cross on her GPS.

Disobeying a direct order like this might mean her job, her entire future.

But she had no choice.

She only hoped she could make it there and back before it was too late.

CHAPTER TWENTY FIVE

Stupid.

The word ricocheted in his head as he passed the intersection of Highway 32 and State Route 411.

Stupid.

If he needed any proof that God was on his side, it came in the timing of it all. He had been headed for the site of the fourth murder—what would become his fourth city—when he saw the police car heading down State Route 411. When he saw it, he kept heading straight down Highway 32, his heart hammering in his chest.

Maybe it was just a coincidence. Maybe the cop was on routine patrol, looking for speeding drivers.

Or maybe they had found the pole. He knew they were investigating him; he'd seen the Scarecrow Killer stories in the papers but had not bothered to read them or watch the snippets about his work on television. He was not doing this for the attention or publicity. He was doing this to spread God's wrath, and to teach the world about love, mercy, and purity.

Of course, the police would not understand this. And if they had found the site that had been destined to raise up his fourth city, it could be over for him. He would not be able to finish his work and that would not please God.

The fourth site would have to change. Maybe it would help him, in the long run. Perhaps the police would be so preoccupied with trying to find him at this fourth site that he could finish out his work elsewhere without risk of being caught.

He came to a convenience store on Highway 32 and turned his truck around in the parking lot. He headed back toward the intersection and passed through without giving State Route 411 a passing glance.

With his sacrifice already chosen and readied, he could still build his fourth city tonight, as he had planned.

He would continue his work elsewhere.

*

She opened her eyes and a flare of pain exploded in her head. She cried out and found that her voice sounded odd—muffled, almost. She tried lifting her hand to her mouth but realized she was unable to do so. She realized there was a cloth gag over her mouth, tied tightly and cutting into the corners of her mouth.

She blinked rapidly, trying to make the pain in her head go away. As her eyes started to focus and the haze of grogginess departed, she started to get a sense of where she was. She was on a hardwood floor that was layered with dust. Her arms were tied behind her back and her ankles were also tied together. She had been stripped to her underwear.

It was this last fact that brought everything slamming back into her memory. A man had come out of nowhere last night as she had gotten home. It had been four o'clock and she had…God, what *had* she done?

But the bright pink bra she was wearing made it impossible to forget what she had done last night. She had tried her best to convince herself that an *escort* was different from what those *other* women did. She was classier, more controlled.

But at the end of the day, she'd done the same thing those other women did. She'd been paid handsomely (hey, fifteen hundred dollars for an hour and a half of "work" wasn't too shabby) and afterwards had not felt as bad as she'd expected to.

But then there had been that man, coming out of the shadows. He'd only said *hello* and then his arm had wrapped around her neck. She'd smelled something for a moment and as she had slipped into blackness, she heard him whispering into her ear about sacrifices and bitter waters.

And now she was here. Her panties were still on and there was no pain, so she was pretty sure she hadn't been raped. But still, she was in trouble.

She tried getting to her knees but every time she came close, her tied ankles made her tip over, slamming her shoulder into the floor. She lay there, weeping, and tried to remember the last thing the man had said to her before whatever he had placed to her nose and mouth had pulled her under.

Slowly, she remembered it. And surprisingly, the lunacy of it made her want to sag and give up rather than figure a way out of this.

Don't worry, he said. *I will build a city for you.*

CHAPTER TWENTY SIX

It took Mackenzie a little over an hour to reach Holy Cross Catholic School, pushing ninety the whole way. School had let out for the day by the time she arrived, and as she hurried up the stairs and was guided by the receptionist, she found she had caught the principal at a good time of day.

The principal was a rotund lady who filled just about every stereotype Mackenzie had ever had about nuns. Warm and inviting at first, Principal Ruth-Anne Costello was all business and rather curt once Mackenzie was in the woman's office and taking a seat at the front of her desk.

"We've heard rumblings about this so-called Scarecrow Killer," Principal Costello said. "Is that why you've come here?"

"It is," Mackenzie said. "How did you know that?"

Principal Costello frowned, but it was the sort of frown that held more anger than disappointment. Mackenzie thought it was a frown that could be found on most staff members at any given time of the day in a school like this one.

"Well, those poor women are strung up on wooden poles and flogged, correct? The religious symbolism is unmistakable. And whenever a killer does his work in the name of terribly misguided religious principles or a warped and misguided interpretation of religion, it is *always* the private religious schools that are put under a microscope."

Mackenzie could only nod. She knew that this was true; she'd seen it several times since she had started working toward her career as a freshman in college. But her silence also came from the fact that Principal Costello was right: the religious undertones to the Scarecrow Killer's actions *were* obvious. Mackenzie had felt it herself when they had found the first body. So why the hell had she ignored them?

Because I was afraid to voice it to Nelson and Porter out of fear of being wrong and then promptly ridiculed, she thought.

But now she had a chance to correct that ignorance and she'd be damned if she was going to let it go to waste.

"Well," Mackenzie said, "we do have a very specific profile. I was hoping that if I could speak to you or maybe someone that has been here for a long time, I could maybe find a potential suspect. And even if not a suspect, maybe someone that knows something about the killings."

"Well," Costello said, "I've been here for thirty-five years. I was a guidance counselor first and then became the principal, a position I've held for nearly twenty years."

She stood up and walked to the left side of her office where a row of ancient-looking filing cabinets lined the wall. "You know," Costello said, "you aren't the first detective to come sniffing around when a crime is committed that seems to have religious influence. Not by a long shot."

Costello pulled four folders from the cabinet and brought them back to the desk. She plopped them down on the desk with enough force to show that she was clearly irritated. Mackenzie reached out to scoop them up but Costello's hand was already pointing to them. Without looking at Mackenzie, Costello started talking again, tapping at each folder with her plump index finger.

"This one," she said, pointing to the first folder, "is Michael Abner. When he was here in the early seventies, he assaulted a girl on the playground and was caught masturbating in the girl's restroom in fifth grade. However, he died in 1984. A terrible car accident, I believe. So he's clearly not a suspect."

With that, Costello removed Michael Abner's folder from the desk. She then promptly eliminated two other folders, as one of them had died five years ago from lung cancer and another had spent his life in a wheelchair—obviously not the sort of person that could cart around wooden poles to murder scenes.

"This last one," Costello said, "belongs to Barry Henderson. While attending Holy Cross, he got into several fights, one of which sent two boys to the emergency room. When he returned from his expulsion, he began sending the teachers dirty letters, an activity which culminated in his attempted rape of the school art teacher while singing his mother's favorite hymn. This happened in 1990. I regret to inform you, though, that he cannot be your suspect either. He has been a resident of the Westhall Home for the Criminally Insane for the last twelve years."

Mackenzie made a mental note to verify that, then watched as Costello placed the folders back into her cabinet. When she closed it, she gave it a little slam that filled the office like a bomb.

"And those are the only students you've had in the last thirty-five years that would be capable of crimes like the Scarecrow Killer is committing?"

"We have no possible way of knowing that," Costello said. "With all due respect, we do not keep tabs on every student that has the potential for a life of crime. That would involve detailed reports on every child that breaks even the slightest rule. The four I just showed you were the most extreme cases, and I have had those on hand for the last several years because it saves a great deal of time when we are approached by the police, especially when they have come up with what they believe are fitting profiles. They always want to blame religion for crimes they cannot solve on their own."

"There's no blame here," Mackenzie said.

"Of course there is," Costello said. "Tell me, Detective. Have you come here to simply find the name of a suspect or what sort of religious doctrine warped them so badly that they are now committing these horrible acts?"

"I don't care *how* the information comes," Mackenzie snapped. "I just need to find out who is killing these women. The *why* is secondary at this point."

Mackenzie started to feel idiotic for coming to Holy Cross. What had she been expecting, anyway? A nice and tidy solution? An old student that matched Ellington's profile to a tee?

"Thank you for your time, Mrs. Costello," she said softly. She got up and headed for the door. As her hand fell on the knob, she was stopped by Principal Costello.

"Why do you think that is, Detective White?"

"What?"

"Why does law enforcement come looking for answers from religion when they can't solve what they believe are faith-based crimes?"

"It just matches the profiles in most cases," Mackenzie said.

"Does it?" Costello asked. "Or is it because humans can't accept evil for what it really is? And because we can't accept it, we have to find something just as intangible to blame it on?"

A question rose to her lips, one that she was unable to bite back before it came out.

"What *is* evil, Ms. Costello? What does evil look like?"

Principal Costello grinned thinly. It was a haunting grin, an expression that hinted at some sort of dark understanding.

"Evil looks like you. It looks like me. We live in a fallen world, Detective. Evil is everywhere."

The doorknob under Mackenzie's hand suddenly felt very cold. She nodded and took her leave, not bothering to look back at Principal Costello for a goodbye.

As she made her way down the labyrinthine halls of Holy Cross, her cell phone buzzed in her pocket. She retrieved it and saw Nelson's name and number on the display. Her heart fell.

The killer, she thought. *He showed up while I was away and Nelson is going to have my ass for it.*

She answered the call with a knot of fear in her stomach. "Hey, Chief."

"White," he said. "Where are you?"

"Holy Cross Catholic School," she said. "I'm following up on Ellington's profile."

Nelson was quiet for a moment as he considered this. "We can go over why the hell you'd defy my order and waste time going there later," he said. "For now, I need you to swing by the station on your way back through."

"But what about Route 411?" she asked. "I'd like to get back out before rush hour."

"Another reason you had no business wasting time following up on Ellington's lead. Just come here now."

"Is everything okay?" she asked.

But Nelson had already ended the call, leaving Mackenzie to listen to nothing more than a dead line.

CHAPTER TWENTY SEVEN

Her sense of unease grew even larger when Mackenzie walked into the station and saw Nancy sitting at the front desk. When Mackenzie came in, Nancy gave her only a brief smile and then looked back down to her desk. This was extremely uncharacteristic for Nancy, a woman who usually seemed to stretch her face to accommodate a smile for anyone that came in the station's front doors.

Mackenzie nearly asked Nancy if she knew what was going on but decided not to. The last thing she wanted was to seem weak and out of the loop as she tried to spearhead the closing to this case. So she bypassed the front desk and headed to the back, marching dutifully toward Nelson's office.

She opened the door and stepped in, trying to appear confident and as if she were fully in control. But even now, as she closed the door behind her, she knew that taking two and a half hours out of her afternoon to visit Holy Cross had been a mistake. She'd been jumping at shadows in an attempt to be as perfect as possible, making sure she exhausted every opportunity, especially ones offered by impressive FBI agents, to get to the bottom of this case.

Nelson looked up to her and for the briefest of moments, an anxious expression crossed his face.

"Have a seat, White," Nelson said, nodding to the chairs on the opposite side of his cluttered desk.

"What's going on?" she asked. The nerves were evident in her voice but that was the last thing on her mind as Nelson seemed to size her up.

"We've got a problem," he said. "And you are not going to like the solution. Our scum-sucking friend Ellis Pope has lodged a formal complaint against you. For now, he's keeping it quiet—just between us and his lawyer. But he says if immediate action isn't taken, he'll take it to the papers. Usually I wouldn't even care about such a threat, but the papers and even some of the television media have painted you as the head of this investigation. If Pope goes to the media with his complaint, things are going to get *very* bad."

"Sir, I was acting on impulse," Mackenzie pleaded. "A mysterious figure was lurking at the edge of a murder scene. It was private property. He was trespassing. He then took off suspiciously. Was I supposed to just let him run? All I did was stop him. I didn't assault him."

He frowned.

"White, I'm on your side on this. One hundred percent. But there's another factor that I can't get past. The State PD is involved now. They caught wind of the confrontation with Pope, too. There's also the fact that you were MIA when they showed up to the scene on State Route 411 this afternoon. I'm pissed about that one myself. But they saw it as sloppy work on your part. Not a good impression."

He raised a hand before she could talk.

"As if that wasn't enough, I got a call from Ruth-Anne Costello about half an hour ago. She complained about your being rude and aggressive. She, too, lodged a complaint."

"Are you *serious*?"

Nelson looked depressed as he nodded his head.

"Yes, unfortunately, I am. Add all of that up and we get a shit storm."

"So what do we do to fix this?" she asked. "What is Pope asking for to stay quiet? How can we appease the State and make the nun happy?"

Nelson sighed and then sneered toward the ceiling, making it apparent that he was not happy with what he was about to say.

"It means that effective immediately, I have to take you off of the Scarecrow Killer case."

Mackenzie felt her skin grow cold. The thought of the killer out there, continuing to kill, and her being unable to try to stop it, was just too much for her.

She didn't know what to say.

Nelson's frown deepened.

"I went to bat for you and tried to get them to ease up," he said. "I even tried to simply let them allow you to finish up this case and then get expelled for a week or so. But Pope and the State PD weren't having it. My hands are tied on this one. I'm sorry."

Mackenzie felt fury replacing the fear that had been boiling up in her stomach. Her first instinct was to lash out at Nelson but she could tell that he was pretty angry about this turn of events, too. Plus, given the way he had been showing her more respect in these last few days, she didn't doubt him when he said he had tried everything he could.

This was not his fault. If anyone was to blame, it was Ellis Pope. And, quite possibly, she herself as well. Ever since she'd heard that creaky floorboard three nights ago, she'd not been herself. Things going askew with Ellington had not helped, either.

Yes, this was mostly on her. And that was perhaps the worst thing of all.

"So who handles the case now?" Mackenzie asked.

"The State Police. And they've got the FBI on stand-by if they're needed. But being that we think we have the exact location of where the killer is coming next, we're hoping it's going to be a pretty simple case."

"Sir, I don't even…"

She stopped here, not knowing what to say. She had never been much of a crier, but she was so angry as she sat in Nelson's office that her body seemed to have no other way to express it other than the threat of tears.

"I know," he said. "This sucks. But when it's all said and done—when this asshole is behind bars and the paperwork is being done—I'm going to make sure your name is all over it in the best ways possible. You have my word on that, White."

She stood up in a state of shock, looking to the door as if it might transport her to some magical world where this conversation had never happened.

"So what am I supposed to do now?" she asked.

"Go home. Get drunk. Do whatever you need to do to shake this off. And when the case is closed, I'll call you and let you know. The State won't care about this ordeal once the killer is arrested. Ellis Pope will be all we have to worry about and that should be easy once you're not in the spotlight."

She opened the door and stepped out.

"I'm sorry as hell, White," he said before she closed the door. "I really am."

She could only nod as she closed the door behind him.

She made her way through the hallway, keeping her eyes on the floor so she would not have to look anyone she passed in the eye. As she made her way out to the front of the station, she looked up to Nancy. Nancy, apparently assuming that Mackenzie was now in the know, gave her a polite frown.

"You okay?" Nancy asked.

"I will be," Mackenzie said, not knowing if it was true or not.

CHAPTER TWENTY EIGHT

While the idea of getting drunk was certainly an enticing one, it also reminded her of what had happened the last time she'd had a drink. Yes, it had only been yesterday but the embarrassment of what had happened made it seem like it had happened years ago and had haunted her all of the time in between. So rather than drink her anger away, Mackenzie did the only other thing she knew to do.

She went home and placed all of the files concerning the Scarecrow Killer on her coffee table. She brewed a pot of coffee and went over every scrap she had on the case. While part of her felt that having the fourth murder site on lockdown was a sure-fire way to an arrest, her instinct told her that the killer would be smart. All it would take was him seeing the merest sign of a police presence to change his plans. Nelson and the State PD likely realized this, too but the fact that they were so close now might make them a little too conservative in their approach.

Outside, night had fallen. She stared out of her blinds for a moment, wondering how the events of the last few days might affect the course of her life. She thought of Zack and realized, for perhaps the first time, that she was glad he was gone. If she was being honest with herself, she'd only tolerated the relationship so she wouldn't be alone—something she had feared ever since walking into her parents' bedroom and finding her dead father.

She also wondered what Ellington was doing. His call with the profile earlier was proof that he was still involved in the Scarecrow Killer case, even if it was only in a background capacity. Thinking of him, she also wondered if she would have taken the profile and the visit to Holy Cross so seriously if it had come from anyone else. Had she been trying to impress him or had she been trying to impress Nelson?

As she looked back to the files in front of her, a very simple yet provocative thought filled her head: *Why impress anyone? Why not just do a good job and work to the best of my abilities? Why care what anyone else thinks of me, much less a useless ex-boyfriend, chauvinist supervisors, or a married FBI agent?*

As if provoked by such thoughts, her cell phone rang. She picked it up from the clutter of files and folders on her coffee table and saw that it was Ellington. She smirked at the phone and almost didn't answer it. He was probably calling to receive thanks for the rabbit trail of Holy Cross, or maybe he had some other insightful idea that would lead her astray and get her reprimanded. If she'd had a clearer head in that moment, she would have ignored the call. But, as it was, some of the fury from Nelson's office was still lurking in her heart and demanded that she answer it.

"Hello, Agent Ellington," she said.

"Hey there, White. I know I keep bothering you, but I'm wrapping up for the day and wanted to see if anything on that profile panned out for you."

"No, it didn't," Mackenzie said, skipping the niceties. "In fact, it seems that the only thing my visit to a Catholic school did was piss off the head nun."

Ellington clearly hadn't been expecting such a response; the other end of the line was quiet for a full five seconds before he responded.

"What happened?" he asked.

"It was a dead end. And while I was there being lectured by the principal on the nature of evil, the State police showed up on the scene of what we believe is going to be the site of the fourth murder. Being that I was not there, they pulled rank."

"Ah, shit."

"Oh, it gets better," Mackenzie snapped. "Remember Ellis Pope?"

"Yeah, the reporter."

"Yes, him. Well, he decided to press charges today with the threat of going to the media about our little scuffle. The State boys heard about that, too. So they got after Nelson and, as of about an hour ago, I was officially removed from this case."

"Are you kidding me?" he asked.

His disbelief sparked even more anger in her and, fortunately, it helped her to realize that she was being rude for no reason. The spot she found herself in was not his fault. All he was doing was checking in and lending a sympathetic ear.

"No, I'm not kidding," she said, trying to keep herself in check. "I have been asked to sit idly by while the good old boys wrap this one up."

"That's not fair."

"I agree," she said. "But I know that Nelson had no choice."

"So what can I do?" Ellington asked.

"Not much, I'm afraid. If you really want to help with the case some more, call Nelson. You may actually get in trouble over talking to me about it."

"White, I'm really sorry about this."

"It is what it is," she said.

Silence filled the line again and this time she didn't give Ellington a chance to pick the conversation back up. If he did, she was afraid her misplaced anger might resurface and he certainly didn't deserve that.

"I've got to go," she said. "Take care."

"Are you going to be okay?" he asked her.

"Yeah," she said. "It's just been a shock."

"Well, take care."

"Thanks."

She ended the call without waiting for a response. She tossed the phone back down on the table next to photocopied pages of the Biblical passages they had deciphered from the posts. She read them over and over again but found nothing new. She then looked to the map taken from the back of the Bible and a crude map that Nancy had made, listing all potential murder sites. It seemed so well put together and simple.

And that was why it made Mackenzie uncomfortable. That's why she felt the need to keep digging, to uncover some truth that they had not yet found. She drank coffee and pored over the files as if it were another day at the office, losing herself in her work despite being off the case.

*

When her cell phone buzzed again, the display on the clock read 7:44. She blinked her eyes and rubbed at her head, slightly in shock. Nearly two hours had passed between Ellington's call and this call but it hadn't felt nearly that long.

She was confused when she saw Nelson's name on the display. She let out a coarse little laugh as she picked up the phone, wondering what else she might have done that would warrant further punishment.

She answered, her eyes once again traveling to the window and the night outside. Was the killer out there, ready to string up his next victim? Or was he already in the act?

"You're about the last person I expected to hear from," Mackenzie said.

"White, I need you to shut your mouth and listen very closely to me," Nelson said. His voice was soft and almost gentle, something she had never heard out of him before.

"Okay," she said, unsure of how to take his tone and instruction.

"Twenty minutes ago, Officer Patrick pulled a man over on State Route 411. He was driving an old red Toyota pickup truck. There was a Bible in the passenger seat and strands of rope in the floorboard. This man, Glenn Hooks, is a pastor at a small Baptist church in the town of Bentley. Here's the kicker: there were eight passages marked in his Bible. One of them dealt with the Six Cities of Refuge."

"My God," Mackenzie breathed.

"Patrick has not arrested this man yet, but was pretty insistent that the man come to the station. He put up a stern argument, but Patrick has him right now. As they're on the way, I'm sending another unit to his house to see if they find anything suspicious."

"Okay," was all Mackenzie could manage to say again.

"The State PD knows nothing about this," Nelson went on. "Between you and I, that's at my instruction. I wanted first crack at this guy before the State got involved. I just got off the phone with Patrick. They'll be here at the station in about ten minutes. I want you here to question the guy. And I need you to do it quickly because I don't know how long we can keep the boys from State in the dark. You *might* have twenty or thirty minutes before I'll need to get you out of here."

"After everything you told me in your office, do you really think that's the best idea?"

"No, it's not a good idea," Nelson said. "But it's all I have right now. I know I sent you packing less than five hours ago, but I'm not asking if you'll do this, I'm telling you. You're still *officially* off the case. That doesn't change. This is being done under the table. I need you on this, White. You got it?"

She'd never felt so disrespected yet valued at the same time. Her heart was sparked by a stirring of excitement but it was underpinned by the anger that had been pushing her for most of the afternoon.

Remember, she thought. *This isn't about impressing anyone. This isn't about being right or wrong or looking good. This is about doing your job and putting a man that tortures and kills women behind bars.*

"White?" Nelson snapped.

She looked down at the coffee table and saw the photos. The women that had been stripped of their dignity, terrorized, beaten and killed. She owed them justice. She owed their families some sort of rest.

Gripping the phone tightly and with a look of steeled determination coming over her face, Mackenzie said:

"I'll be there in fifteen minutes."

CHAPTER TWENTY NINE

When Mackenzie arrived at the station, there were two officers at the front doors waiting for her. She was surprisingly pleased to see that one of them was Porter. He gave her a knowing smile as she reached the doors and without a word, the men opened the doors and led her inside. They had taken three steps into the station when Mackenzie realized that Porter and the other officer were acting as a shield. They walked to either side of her at a brisk pace, helping her to blend in just in case anyone at the station saw her and might want to stir up trouble.

Quickly, they reached the main hall where she saw Nelson standing outside of the interrogation room. He straightened up when he saw them coming and Mackenzie saw that he looked terribly on edge—like he might very well blast off like a rocket at any moment.

"Thanks," he said when they reached him.

"Of course," Mackenzie said.

Nelson gave Porter and the other officer a curt nod and they headed away at once. After taking a single step, though, Porter turned back to her and whispered. "Damn fine work," he said with the same smile he'd showed her at the front door.

She only nodded her head in response, returning the smile. With that, the officers headed down the hall, back toward the front of the building.

"Okay," Nelson said. "This Hooks guy, he's being mostly cooperative. He's just scared and nervous. He's doing a great deal of talking and hasn't asked to see a lawyer yet. So don't push him too hard and we might get out of this one without a lawyer coming and stalling everything."

"Okay."

"We'll be watching in the review room so if anything goes wrong, someone can be in there in less than ten seconds. You good?"

"Yeah, I'm good."

Nelson gave her a reassuring pat on the back and then opened the door for her. To her surprise, Nelson walked away from the room, down the hall toward the review room. Mackenzie looked to the open door for a moment before walking in.

He's in there, she thought. *The Scarecrow Killer is in there.*

When she entered the interrogation room, the man at the small table in the center of the room went through a strange series of emotions; first he sat up as rigid as a board, then a frown washed over his face, followed by confusion and then ultimately a vague sort of relief.

Mackenzie went through a similar range of emotions when she saw the killer for the first time. He looked to be in his early fifties, his hair gray around the edges and the lines of age starting to show in his face. He was a skinny man but rather tall. He regarded her with deep brown eyes that were easy to read: he was sacred and deeply confused.

"Hi, Mr. Hooks," she said. "My name is Detective White. I think if you can answer some questions for me as honestly as you can, you can get out of here pretty quickly. I'm told you've been cooperative so far, so let's keep that up, okay?"

He nodded. "This is all some huge understanding," Hooks said. "They think I killed three women. They think I'm that Scarecrow Killer."

"You're not?" she asked.

"Of course I'm not! I'm a pastor at Grace Creek Baptist Church."

"That's what I'm told," Mackenzie said. "The Bible in your truck was marked to several passages. One of them happens to be closely associated with the Scarecrow Killer case."

"Yes, that's what the other officers have said. The Cities of Refuge, correct?"

Mackenzie took a moment to regroup. She was pissed that someone had already revealed their hand and told Hooks about the Cities of Refuge connection. She was going to have to try a different angle here. All she knew for certain was that her gut told her implicitly that Hooks was certainly not the Scarecrow Killer. The fear in his eyes was genuine and, as far as she was concerned, told them all they needed to know.

"What about the strands of rope we found in the floorboard?"

"Grace Creek's Vacation Bible School is in two weeks," Hooks said. "The strands of rope were left over from one of the stage decorations we're creating. We're going with a jungle theme this year and we used the rope for vines and a little mock swinging bridge."

"And where is Grace Creek Baptist located?"

"On Highway 33."

"And that runs parallel to Stare Route 411, correct?"

"It does."

Mackenzie had to turn her back to Hooks for a moment to hide the expression on her face. How had Nelson and his sycophant

135

officers been so blind and stupid? Had they not done *any* digging before bringing this poor man in?

When she managed to compose herself, she turned back to him, trying her best not to show him that she was already convinced that he was not the killer. "Why, exactly, did you have the passage about the Cities of Refuge marked?"

"I'm planning to preach about it in three or four weeks."

"Can I ask why?" Mackenzie asked.

"It's to talk about committing sin in a way that doesn't make the congregation feel guilty. We all sin, you know. Even me. Even the most devout. But many people are raised to believe that sin means eternal damnation and the cities are a great illustration for God's forgiveness of sin. They are all about *degree* of sin. They were meant primarily for those who had committed *unintentional* murder. Not all sins are the same. And even those who commit murder, if unintentional, can be forgiven."

Mackenzie thought about this for a moment, feeling a connection trying to click in her head. There was something there, but it wasn't making itself known just yet.

"One final question, Mr. Hooks," she said. "Your Toyota is rather old. How long have you owned it?"

Hooks thought for a moment and shrugged. "Eight years or so. I brought it used from a member of Grace Creek."

"Have you ever hauled any sort of wood in it?"

"Yes. I had several sheets of plywood in it last week for more decorations. And from time to time, I help people gather firewood in the winter and deliver it to their homes."

"Anything bigger than that?"

"No. Not that I can remember."

"Thank you very much, Mr. Hooks. You've been very helpful. I feel pretty confident that you'll be out of here in no time."

He nodded, as confused as ever. Mackenzie gave him a final look as she left the room, closing the door behind him. The moment she was outside of the interrogation room, Nelson came out of the review room a few doors down. He looked flustered as he approached her and she could feel the tension coming off of him in waves.

"Well, that was quick," he said.

"He's not the killer," Mackenzie said.

"And how the hell are you so sure?" he asked.

"With all due respect, sir, did you even ask him about the rope?"

136

"We did," Nelson snapped. "He spouted off some story about needing it for Vacation Bible School at his church."

"Did anyone bother to check on that?"

"I'm waiting on a call at any moment," he said. "I sent a car out there about half an hour ago."

"Sir, his church is about fifteen minutes away from the site in question. He said he had plans to preach on the Cities of Refuge sometime soon."

"Seems convenient, doesn't it?"

"It does," she said. "But when is such a weak connection grounds for an arrest?"

Nelson scowled at her and placed his hands on his hips. "I knew it was a mistake to bring you in. Are you *determined* to draw this out as long as you can? Do you want the attention so you can stay in the headlines?"

Mackenzie couldn't help herself when she took a step forward, her anger rising up. "Please tell me that's just the frustration talking," she said. "I'd like to think you have a better head on your shoulders than to think such a thing."

"Check your tone, Mackenzie," he said. "Right now, you're just off this case. Get in my face again, I'll suspend you indefinitely."

A tense silence fell between them that lasted only three seconds, interrupted by the ringing of Nelson's cell phone. He broke his gaze with Mackenzie, turned his back to her, and answered it.

Mackenzie stood there and listened to his end of the conversation, hoping whatever the call was about, it might help to clear things up and free Pastor Hooks.

"What is it?" Nelson asked, his back still turned. "Yeah? Okay....you're certain? Well shit. Yeah...got it."

When Nelson turned back to her, he looked like he wanted to throw his cell phone down the hall. His cheeks had taken on a bright red color and he looked absolutely defeated.

"What is it?" Mackenzie asked.

Nelson hesitated, looking to the ceiling and letting out a sigh. It was very much the posture of someone that was about to eat a large helping of humble pie.

"The rope in his truck is an exact match to rope used to create stage designs for Vacation Bible School at Grace Creek Baptist. More than that, there were printed papers and handwritten notes in a small office in the back of the church that show where Hooks is indeed planning a sermon on the Cities of Refuge."

It took every ounce of her will to not make a comment about how he and his officers had been wrong—how they had been so eager to wrap this case up without the help of the State or the FBI that they had arrested a man that had no business ever being cuffed.

"So he's good to go?" Mackenzie said.

"Yes. He checks out."

She allowed herself a thin smile. "Should you tell him, or should I?"

Nelson looked like his head might explode at any moment. "You do it," he said. "And when you're done, please promptly get the hell out of here. It might be best that you and I don't speak for a day or so."

Gladly, she thought.

She turned back to the interrogation room, glad to be out of Nelson's sight. When she closed the door behind her, Hooks looked up to her with hope in those dark brown eyes.

"You're free to go."

He nodded appreciatively, breathed deeply, and said: "Thank you."

"Do you mind if I ask you one more question before you go?" she asked.

"That would be fine."

"Why would God designate cities for sinners to escape to? Isn't it sort of God's job to punish sinners?"

"That's up for debate. My own belief is that God wanted to see his children succeed. He wanted to allow them the chance to get right with him."

"And these sinners believed they could find God in these cities? They thought they could find favor with him there?"

"In a way, yes. But they also knew that God is at the center of all things. It was just up to them to seek Him. And these cities were the designated places for them to do that."

Mackenzie chewed this over as she headed for the door. She walked Hooks through the motions of checking out but her mind was elsewhere. She thought about six cities located in a circle and how a sometimes wrathful but ultimately forgiving God oversaw it all.

How had Hooks put it?

But they also knew that God is at the center of all things.

Suddenly, Mackenzie felt as if a filter had been removed from her mind's eye. With that single comment floating in her head, the connection she had nearly made in the interrogation room snapped into place.

Five minutes later, she was speeding back home, letting that single thought wash over every corner of her mind.

God is at the center of all things.

The clock on her dashboard read 8:46, but Mackenzie knew her night was just getting started.

Because, if she was correct, she knew how to find where the killer lived.

CHAPTER THIRTY

As soon as she returned home, Mackenzie immediately went to the couch and hurried to the clutter of paperwork she had left on the coffee table. It was ironic in a way; she'd thought the house would be tidier after Zack had left, but instead, her work clutter had replaced his mess. For just a moment, she wondered where he was and what he was doing. But the thought lasted only a handful of seconds. It was replaced by the thought that had escorted her home, still whirling through her head like a stray breeze across a desert floor.

God is at the center of all things.

She scoured through the papers on the table and came to the two maps—the Old Testament Cities of Refuge map and the local one showing the area within one hundred miles. She overlaid them against one another and looked at them contemplatively. She then focused on the local map and stared at the Xs she had placed there with a black Sharpie, tracing them with her finger. She then encompassed the Xs, connecting them all with a line and drawing the implied circle that the locations made.

With the circle drawn, she turned her attention to the inside of the circle. Grabbing the nearest pen, she traced a faint line from each of the six "cities" like spokes on a wheel from the edges of the circle.

God is at the center of all things.

The lines all met in the center of the circle. She drew another, much smaller circle where all of the lines connected. It encompassed a section of the downtown district not too far away from where they had apprehended Clive Traylor a few days ago. Along the very edge of this new smaller circle she saw the squiggly line that indicated a river—in this case, Danvers River, the little waterway that etched its way through a park downtown, along the backside of several rundown downtown properties and then eventually emptied out into Sapphire Lake.

It was hard to tell from the map, but she was pretty sure her new circle included two or three different streets and a small cluster of forest that separated the western downtown region from the edge of Sapphire Lake.

This was the center of the killings—the central point that existed between the killer's sites, so-called cities. If this man felt that he was, in a way, God, or working under the guidance of God, then he probably thought he existed in the center of it all. And if

God was at the center of all things, this central point was very likely his home.

She simply sat there for a moment, a familiar twinge of excitement starting to bloom in her heart. She knew she had a decision to make and that it could very well decide the outcome of her career. She could call Nelson and give him this bit of information, but she was pretty sure he wouldn't take her call. And even if he took her seriously, she feared that the idea would be placed on the back burner.

The site they had discovered with the pole already in place meant that the killer had been on the verge of striking again. What if he already had a woman ready for his next sacrifice? And what if he had to think outside of the box since his other three murder sites were under surveillance?

To hell with it, she thought.

Mackenzie jumped to her feet, brushing much of the paperwork off of the table in her hurry and excitement. She went into the bedroom to retrieve her service pistol and as she holstered it to her belt, her cell phone rang. The sudden and unexpected sound of it made her jump slightly and she had to take a moment to calm her nerves before answering it. Looking at the display, she saw that it was Ellington again.

"Hello?" she asked.

"Oh wow," Ellington said. "I wasn't expecting you to answer. I was just going to leave a message letting you know I was turning in for the night and for you to call me tomorrow with news on the arrest. Are you not there yet?"

"Oh, I've gone and already come back. It wasn't the killer."

He paused.

"And you found that out in less than half an hour?"

"Yes. It was obvious. Nelson and his men, they, well, they weren't exactly on top of things."

"Too eager to make an arrest?"

"Something like that," she said as she finished holstering the gun.

"You okay?" Ellington asked. "You sound really rushed."

She almost didn't tell him—she almost kept her new theory quiet. If she turned out to be wrong on this, it could turn out very badly—especially if someone knew what she was up to beforehand. Yet, on the other hand, she felt that she was *not* wrong; she felt it in her heart, her gut, her bones. And if she *was* missing something or jumping to conclusion, Ellington was the most logical person she knew.

"White?"

"I think I figured something out," Mackenzie said. "About the killer. About where he lives."

"What?" He sounded shocked. "How's that?"

She quickly told him about her conversation with Pastor Hooks and how she had located the center of things with the map. As she spoke it out loud, she became ever more convinced that this was it. This was finally the right path that would lead them to the killer.

When she was done, there was silence on the line for a moment. She braced herself, expecting the usual criticism she always received.

"You think it's flawed?" she asked.

"No. Not at all. I think it's genius."

She was surprised herself, and felt motivated.

"What did Nelson say?" he asked.

"I haven't called him. I'm not going to."

"You have to," he urged.

"No I don't. He doesn't want me on the case. And after the exchange we had at the station, I doubt he'd even take my call."

"Well then let me shoot the lead to the State guys."

"Too risky," she said. "If it turns out to be a dead end, who does the blame come back to? You? Me? Either scenario would not be good."

"That's true," Ellington said. "But what if it's *not* a dead end? What if you apprehend the killer? You'll have to call Nelson anyway."

"But at least I'll have results. And as long as I catch the bastard, I really don't care what my consequences are."

"Look," he said sounding frustrated, "you can't do this. Not alone."

"I have to," she said. "We have no idea when he's going to kill again. I can't sit on this until Nelson is ready to talk to me again or until your guys decide it's worth their time to come down here."

"I could present the idea as my own," Ellington said. "Maybe that would speed things up on the Bureau end."

"I thought of that," Mackenzie said. "But when's the soonest you'd have agents out here?"

His sigh from the other end told her he knew she was right.

"Probably about five or six hours," he answered. "And that's being optimistic."

"So you see my point."

"And you see how you're putting me in an awkward position," he countered. "If you go out there and something happens to you, I *have* to say something to my supervisor. If you get harmed or killed and it's discovered that I knew about your plan, that's my ass on the line."

"I guess I just have to make sure I don't get hurt or killed."

"Damn it, White—"

"Thanks for the concern, Ellington. But this has to be done now."

She ended the call before he could say anything else that might sway her out of her decision. Even now with the call ended, she wondered if this was being too reckless. She'd be on her own, venturing into darkness with specific orders not to get involved in the case. Worse than that, she'd potentially be on the turf of a killer they knew very little about.

She walked through the living room and out the front door before she could change her mind. Breathing in the crisp night air seemed to push aside any doubt. She ran her hand along the shape of the pistol holstered in her belt and it calmed her a bit.

Wasting no more time, she dashed to her car and started the ignition. She peeled out of her driveway and headed west, the night unrolling before her like some dark curtain on a stage that was finally about to open.

CHAPTER THIRTY ONE

She'd listened to him rummaging around in the house all day. On occasion, he'd sing hymns, one of which she knew from sitting on her grandmother's lap in a small pew in a rural Baptist church. She was pretty sure it was called "How Great Thou Art." Each time he hummed it she felt a fresh wave of nausea and fear, knowing what he had done to her—and what he would do.

As she'd listened to his singing and movements, she'd tried to get to her feet again. If she'd had on clothes, it would have been easier. She'd managed to roll to the far wall, place her back against it, and slowly lift herself up. Even then, though, her calves started to stretch and burn due to her ankles being so tightly tied together. Because she had worked up such a sweat by that point, her back would slip against the wall and she'd slip right back to the ground on her backside.

Now, wrists bleeding from the abrasions the ropes had etched into her skin, she backed up against the wall again. Her legs felt like putty and the scratches she'd gotten along her back stung like bee stings. Whimpering, she tried again, pushing against the wall while she pushed herself up by her feet. When she reached the point where her ankles and calves started to burn, she simply forced herself through the pain and extended her legs.

As she stood up fully, her legs wobbled and she almost fell right away. But she pressed against the wall and managed to keep her balance.

Okay, now what?

She didn't know. She was just relieved to finally be on her feet. She figured if she could get through the doorway a few feet to her right, she might be able to find a phone and call the police. She'd heard him open the door and close it all day. She supposed he was going outside for small periods of time and coming back in. If she could get just a glimpse of what was going on elsewhere in the house, maybe she could get out of this alive.

She slunk against the wall and made it to the doorway. Her skin broke out into goose bumps as sweat coated her body. She felt her body trembling and she wanted to cry, to sink back to the floor. She scanned the room, looking for any sharp instrument with which she could sever her wrist ties.

But there was none.

She felt like giving up. This was too much, she though, too hard.

With her back to the door, she fumbled for the doorknob. When she had it in her hands, she turned it slowly. There was a slight *click* as the tumbler removed itself from the doorframe.

She stepped away from the door, letting it slowly swing open. She could feel the fresh air from the other side of the door and she wondered if anything had ever felt so good in her life.

She turned around slowly, trying to move as quietly as she could. She'd find a phone to call someone, or an open window. Sure, her hands and legs were tied up but she'd risk a fall just to get out of here.

But when she fully turned, facing the doorway, he was standing there.

Her scream was blocked by the cloth gag over her mouth. He smiled at her and stepped into the room. He placed a hand on her bare shoulder and caressed her there. Then, with his smile widening, he shoved her. She went sprawling to the ground and when she did, her shoulder bounced awkwardly. She screamed again and it turned into a deep sob.

"You'll be free soon enough," he told her.

He got down on his knees and again placed a hand on her shoulder, as if for reassurance.

"We'll both be free, and it will be glorious."

He left the room and when he closed it, she could hear an additional clicking noise as he set the lock. She wept, feeling like she might suffocate because of the gag. And all the while, he moved around downstairs, singing hymns to the same God that she found herself desperately praying to on his dusty floor.

*

He did not like working under pressure. He also did not like change, especially when things had been so carefully planned and thought out. Yet here he was, having to alter his plans halfway through his work. There were three more cities to raise, three more sacrifices. One was propped and ready to go but he still had no idea how he would carry out the other two.

For now, he had to take it one step at a time. For now, the fourth city was all he was concerned about.

He thought he'd adjusted well in light of recent events. It had been the work of God that he had driven by the planned site of the fourth city just in time to see the police presence. The men of the world were on to him and would do whatever they could to stop his work. But God, sovereign and all-knowing, was protecting him. He had prayed then, and God had told him that it was the work that mattered, not the location of the sacrifice.

He had adjusted accordingly. And he had done well, as far as he was concerned.

For instance, the woman was no longer in the upstairs room, the place he had left her in an hour before. Now, she was in the shed. She was in the fetal position, her arms pulled behind her and her knees drawn up. Her ankles and wrists were bound together, the rope given some slack so she would not accidentally pop her shoulder out of its socket. She had to be unblemished when he put her upon the pole. God would not accept sacrifices with flaws.

He studied her for a moment as he stood against the pole that he had just finished erecting in the shed. This woman was quite pretty, prettier than the others for sure. Her driver's license placed her age at nineteen, and he read she was originally from Los Angeles. He did not know why the woman had come here, but he knew that God had placed her in his path. The girl did not know it, but she should feel honored. She did not realize that she had been selected even before she was born to be sacrificed for the glory of God.

He never bothered trying to explain this to the women. They would not listen.

He had stripped this one completely naked. He'd left the bra and underwear on the others because he did not want to risk temptation. But this one had been such a perfect sacrifice that he could not help himself. He had never seen breasts so perfect, not even in movies or magazines.

He knew he must be punished for looking at her flesh in such a way. He'd be sure to repent of that sin, to hurt himself many times tonight.

After setting up the pole, he'd gone to the hardware store and purchased a roll of plastic covering. He'd spent half an hour covering the floor of the shed with it, using staples rather than nails, as they would be easier to remove later on. Setting up the pole in the shed and then covering the floor with the sheets of plastic had been laborious work, but it had been good for him. In a way, it had made him more appreciative of the sacrifice to come. Working this hard to make way for a sacrifice made him feel more worthy.

He stopped and took a deep breath, admiring his handiwork.

It was almost time now.

He had to pray first and then he would string the woman up. He'd have to tighten the gag because he had never given a sacrifice in such a populated area. One slip and a neighbor would hear her screams as the whip came down. But he would worry about that after she was tied to the pole.

First, prayer and repentance. He needed to pray that his cities—his sacrifices—would be pleasing to God and that his work would exemplify His glory and love for man.

He got to his knees in front of the pole. Before he closed his eyes to pray, he looked to the woman again. Quiet understanding seemed to spread across her face and seeing this, he went into prayer with a great sense of peace.

It was almost as if she knew that there was a great reward waiting for her afterwards, as if she knew she would receive that reward and be released from this world of filth before the hour was through.

CHAPTER THIRTY TWO

Mackenzie parked her car at the end of the block in this dilapidated neighborhood, and pulled up a close-range map of the area on her cell phone before getting out of her car. She knew that her search would consist of a one-block radius along three different streets: Harrison, Colegrove, and Inge.

She knew that Inge Street could be crossed off of her list because the houses along this end of the street were vacant, having been condemned several years ago. She knew this because it was a popular locale for drug deals and gang activity. She'd netted her first drug bust here and had also had to pull her sidearm for the first time in her career just a few streets over.

Colegrove and Harrison streets, though, were fully occupied and managing to hang on in this otherwise deteriorating part of town. These were people with menial jobs that usually spent their paychecks on liquor, lottery tickets, and, if they had money left over, fast food dinners most nights of the week.

Before getting out, she pulled up Ellington's number. She texted him the street names and then signed off with: *If you don't hear from me within a few hours, call someone and send them here.*

She then set her phone to silent and stepped out into the night.

Mackenzie walked down Harrison Street at a steady pace, not wanting to seem overly suspicious at such a late hour even though any single woman walking down these streets after dark would be seen as foolish. She kept an eye out for houses with trucks or vans on the property, and spotted two residences that fit the description.

The first house had a van out front, parked in the small driveway. Worn vinyl lettering along the side of the white van read *Smith Brothers Plumbing.*

Slinking through the shadows as quickly as she could, Mackenzie went to the side of the van and peered into the passenger side window. She could barely see into the back but she did manage to see a corner of a toolbox. In the front, tucked between the seats and console as well as between the dashboard and the windshields, she saw several invoice sheets. On the top of a few, she saw the same artwork that was on the side of the van, marking the invoices as Smith Brothers Plumbing.

With that house eliminated from her search, she moved on to the next house. A black truck sat outside along the curb. It was a newer model, adorned with a *Don't Tread On Me* bumper sticker and a decal in the back glass indicating the owner was a Vietnam vet. She looked into the back of the truck for any sign that it had carried a large cedar pole recently but saw nothing. While she didn't want to rule a vet out just because of their service to the country, Mackenzie did find the thought of a man reaching seventy putting up those poles by himself hard to imagine.

She reached the end of the block and then turned right toward Colegrove Street. She could hear the thumping of thunderous bass from a nearby house blasting rap music. As she passed by each house looking for trucks or vans, she caught glimpses of the murky Danvers River reflecting the moonlight far behind the houses.

There was one truck parked alongside the street right in front of her. Even before she approached it, she saw that it was not the truck she was looking for. The back tires were flat and it showed signs of neglect that made her think it had been given up on years ago.

She was halfway down the street, peering ahead and seeing nothing but cars the rest of the way down, some in scant driveways but most along the curb. There were six in all, one new model among the other five rusted heaps.

She was just starting to feel that she had unraveled yet another unsuccessful theory when she spotted the house on her left. An older model Honda Accord sat along the curb. A small stretch of overgrown front yard led to a badly maintained chain-link fence that extended to an equally poor wooden fence that separated the yard from the neighboring property. She walked further along the property and froze when she got to the opposite side of the house.

The chain-link fence was nowhere to be seen, apparently coming to a closure point in the backyard. What she did see, though, was a makeshift driveway that was nothing more than flattened grass and thin dirt tracks. She followed the tracks with her eyes and saw that they ended where an old green Ford pickup was parked. It sat front end out, the grille and dead headlights staring right at her.

Mackenzie glanced to the house and saw that a single light was on. It cast very little light, making her think it was a lamp or a hallway light from further back in the house.

Moving quickly, she dashed into the yard, following the course of the flattened grass to the truck. She looked into the truck through the driver's side window and saw some old fast food bags and other trash.

Among it all, sitting in the center of the bench-like seat, was a Bible.

With adrenaline pumping into her heart, she reached for the driver's side door. She was not at all surprised when she found it locked.

She went to the back of the truck and saw that the tailgate was down. She peered into it and saw no clear indication of what it had recently carried, though it was hard see anything in the dark.

She looked behind her into the backyard and saw that her assumption had been correct; the chain-link fence ran the length of the yard and then came up and around where it stopped alongside a shed. She could not see any windows, but she could see a trace of light issuing from a space along the shed door.

She stepped into the backyard, inching closer to the chain-link fence. As the shed came into view, she started to think the light was indeed something smaller, a candle, perhaps. With her curiosity now morphing into something very close to caution, she came to the edge of the fence. She crouched low to the ground as she neared the faint glow coming from between the small crack along the door and the frame.

She started to look for a way through the fence, fearing that crawling over it might make too much noise. As she did this, her eyes fell on another shape alongside the shed. She'd missed it before, as it was low to the ground and cloaked in shadows. But now that she was no more than ten feet from the shed, the shape was clear and defined.

Actually, it was two shapes.

Two cedar poles, cut to roughly eight feet in length.

She knew she should wait for backup.

But she sensed, with all that she was, that there was no time.

So, with fire in her muscles and her nerves firing on all cylinders, she reached up and grabbed the chain-link fence.

And then she began to climb.

CHAPTER THIRTY THREE

The fence was old and rusted just like everything else on this godforsaken street. She felt the rust cutting into the padding of her finger but at least, because of the rust, the chain-link material made almost no noise as she scaled it. The fence was seven or eight feet tall and soon she reached the top.

She threw one leg over, steadied herself, and then brought the other over.

With a single push away from the fence, she leaped from the top and landed in the yard with a soft thud.

She instantly withdrew her Glock from its holster and crept toward the shed in a crouching position. She made her way to the door and rose up on her legs a bit, trying to find the warped area in the frame that kept the door from shutting all the way. She found it three quarters of the way up the door and peered inside.

She saw the pole right away, standing directly in the center of the shed. A scurrying shadow flew across it, followed by the object that had cast it. She saw the woman first, her legs kicking at the air, and then the man that was holding her from behind. The woman was naked except for a gag around her mouth. A series of muffled cries were coming from behind it as she fought to get away.

The man was wrestling her toward the pole. A strand of rope was wrapped around his shoulder like a limp snake.

Mackenzie, heart slamming so hard she could barely hear, had seen enough. She knew she'd have to act fast; she had to pull the door open and get inside with her gun raised before the creep had any idea what was happening.

This is where it would be easier with help, she thought to herself, suddenly regretting that she had ventured out here alone.

She extended her hand to the door's rusty handle. When she grasped it, a sickening thought filled her head. *What if it's locked from the inside somehow?*

That answer was simple enough. Now that she was inches away from the killer, she was willing to take more risks. *If that's the case,* she thought, *I'll shoot through the fucking door.*

She gripped the handle and took a deep breath. She held it in and didn't exhale until she had pulled the door open.

She leaped forward, bringing the Glock up.

"Police! Put the weapon down and your hands—"

She knew she'd made a mistake the moment she stepped inside. Something under her feet felt odd. And there came a noise, something that made no sense.

Mackenzie looked down for a split second, her eyes leaving the shape of the man in front of her, and saw the plastic sheeting that covered the floor. She was standing on it. And although it took less than a second for her to process what she was seeing, it was a second too much.

The murky figure in front of her dropped immediately to his haunches, grabbed the plastic sheeting in his hands, and yanked with all he had.

Mackenzie felt the ground move. The plastic she was standing on was yanked toward him and she lost her footing and went airborne.

The man then shoved the naked woman in her direction, and she landed on top of her.

Mackenzie, dazed, reached up and shoved the frantic woman off her, but by the time she did, the man was already lunging for her, bringing his fist down. She was halfway up when it struck Mackenzie directly between the eyes and sent her back to the ground.

As she fell to the ground, Mackenzie got her first glimpse of the killer. He was in his forties and partially bald. His eyes were electric blue and had the look of a crazed animal that has been penned up for far too long and has a pretty good idea of what freedom must be like. He was short but had a stocky look to him. Mackenzie had a pretty good idea that there was more muscle under his shirt than his appearance made it seem. The punch he'd delivered to her was another indication of this.

He was coming in for her now, moving with a quickness that the small space of the shed seemed incapable of containing. He had something in his hand that seemed to slither through the darkness. By the time he had raised his arm, Mackenzie realized what it was. She saw the splintered end sailing toward her.

Mackenzie rolled out of the way just in time.

The whip cracked less than two inches from Mackenzie's right ear. The sound was deafening.

The killer brought the whip back again, this time aiming it directly for Mackenzie.

This time, she reached back, raised her gun, steadied her hands, and fired.

The motion he made as he brought the whip down skewed her aim and the bullet hit him high in the left shoulder rather than his heart.

He dropped the whip and stumbled forward, looking to Mackenzie as if the very idea of a gun was absurd to him.

Still, he was undaunted. He dove for her, going for her gun. Mackenzie fired again, this one grazing his right arm as he came down.

He slammed his full weight on top of her and the jolt of it sent a blast of pain through her body. Her hands opened reflexively and the Glock went to the floor.

The moment she heard the gun hit the floor, the killer rose up and drew his fist back. Before he could bring it down, Mackenzie punched him squarely in the gut. From the floor on her back, she did not get her full force into it, and it only diverted his blow. Yet when he brought it down and his fist only bounced from her shoulder, Mackenzie spun and clubbed him hard in the side of the jaw with her elbow.

He went sliding off of her and she instantly went for the Glock.

The killer ran as Mackenzie's hand found the gun. She brought it up and aimed at the door just as he made his exit. She nearly fired, but the naked woman was in the way.

Mackenzie jumped to her feet and looked over at the naked woman, shaking, still bound.

"Stay here," Mackenzie said. "I'll come back for you."

The woman nodded and Mackenzie saw something broken in the woman's eyes. The events of this night, no matter how they turned out, would traumatize this poor young woman for the rest of her life.

With that haunting thought pushing her, Mackenzie sprinted out of the shed just in time to see the back door to the house closing. Mackenzie gave instant chase, fully expecting the back door to be locked.

When she turned the knob, it did so freely. The back door opened, revealing a small entryway and a darkened kitchen beyond.

He did that on purpose, she thought. *He wants me to follow him inside.*

She gave only a moment's thought before she stepped inside and raised her gun, plunging into darkness.

CHAPTER THIRTY FOUR

Mackenzie stepped into the kitchen and could tell right away that this man did not care much for the way he lived. She smelled spoiled food coming from somewhere, mingled with the smells of dust and old body odor. She felt her palms sweating on her gun as her heart slammed, knowing she could full well die in this house, and she tried to steady them.

Mackenzie crept across the kitchen floor, listening for movement elsewhere in the house. Now that they were inside, she knew that there was no telling what the killer might have access to. At this very instant, he could be getting his own gun.

Mackenzie reached the edge of the kitchen where a dark hallway waited. Halfway down the small hallway, a flight of wooden stairs led to a second floor. The killer had the advantage here and she knew it. It would be foolish to go venturing down that hall. She looked to the right and saw a living room, illuminated by a small lamp on an end table. Another Bible sat on the end table. A bookmark stuck out of it and a pen and pad of paper sat beside it.

From upstairs, the slightest creak of a floorboard sounded out, giving away the killer's position. Mackenzie acted quickly, wanting to get the jump on him.

Now or never, she thought.

She ran down the hallway and halfway up the stairs in less than three seconds. She paused there, staring into the darkness above her. Her eyes were beginning to adjust and when she thought it was safe to do so, she started up the stairs.

She was in mid-step when she heard footsteps in the kitchen. Confused, Mackenzie looked back down the stairs just in time to see the would-be victim coming toward the stairs. Her eyes looked half-tinged with lunacy and something about seeing such an attractive woman in her underwear in the midst of such a tense scene was abstract in a way that befuddled Mackenzie just enough.

"Please," the woman said. "You have to call the police. I can't—"

But she didn't get a chance to finish. She screamed, her eyes now trailing just above Mackenzie. Mackenzie turned just in time to see the killer's shape coming at her, racing down the stairs so quickly that Mackenzie barely had time to raise her gun.

Crack!

He whipped her, and a fierce stinging sensation erupted on her right hand right across the knuckles—followed by a blinding pain that raced along her left cheek as he whipped again.

She felt blood flowing instantly, racing down her fingers and face. She saw him coming at her, diving from the top step. She fired blindly, knowing that the pain in her hand affected her shot.

Still, she heard him cry out in pain, as the shot took him low in the stomach.

Amazingly, the shot only slowed his progress. Once again, his full weight slammed into her and she went falling backwards down the stairs.

She grabbed for the wall, again dropping her gun, but it did no good. They both went falling down the stairs and when Mackenzie's back hit, it exploded in pain and the wind went rushing out of her.

They tumbled down the remainder of the stairs in a bundle of arms and legs. When they finally hit the floor, Mackenzie's back was a spasm of pain and the blood from her face was coating her neck and soaking into her shirt.

The killer was getting to his knees now, drawing back the same whip he had attacked her with on the stairs. He turned and whipped the original object of his madness, the woman in the pink bra, who was standing and gaping, frozen in fear. It slapped her across the shoulder, bringing up a red whelp right away, her blood splashing against the hallway wall.

With the woman falling to the ground and wailing, Mackenzie tried to launch her own attack but her back didn't seem to want to work for a moment. She felt paralyzed and wondered if she had snapped her spine on the way down the stairs.

The killer turned his attention to her and drew back the whip. The smile on his face was a thing of madness, a smile that belonged in asylums and nightmares.

"I will raise a city in your name," he said as he readied himself to bring the whip down on her.

Mackenzie could only flinch, waiting for the whip to come down on her flesh with that sick cracking noise, its barbed end to pierce her flesh and disfigure her for good. She wondered what she would look like when he was done—if she survived at all.

Suddenly, there came a booming noise in the kitchen. Mackenzie didn't understand what it was until she saw a body appear in the hallway. It came racing down the hall and leapt for the killer.

155

The killer, caught in mid-turn, was tackled to the ground. It wasn't until the two bodies started fighting for position on the ground that Mackenzie saw, to her shock, who the other person was.

Porter.

It made no sense. A part of Mackenzie wondered if she had hit her head on the way down the stairs and was seeing things.

But as her back finally started to loosen up, she groggily got to her knees and saw what was happening before her. Porter had saved her. He was now fighting with the killer, positioned on top of him and delivering a deft right hand to the face.

With black dots racing in her vision, Mackenzie looked around for her gun. The floor felt like it was swaying beneath her and she could actually *smell* her own blood now. It was coming out of her cheek in what felt like a river and—

Suddenly, she saw her gun. It was inches from the killer's hand and he was clearly reaching for it.

"Porter," she croaked, still finding her back untrusting and her legs wobbly.

She tried to run forward but her back locked up and she went to her knees in a grimace of pain. She could only look on helplessly as the killer grabbed her Glock.

Porter noticed it just in time, reaching out to stop the killer from getting the gun into position to fire.

But Porter lost his balance atop the killer as he did this and the killer took advantage, rolling away, sending Porter to the floor, and grabbing the gun.

The killer stood and fired.

The gunshot was deafening and the roar of pain from Porter was far too brief. Mackenzie's heart fell, hoping it didn't mean what she thought it did.

Mackenzie pushed past the flaring pain in her back and stumbled forward. The killer stood there, his face now also bloodied from Porter's attack, and Mackenzie attacked him from behind, driving an elbow hard into the space between his shoulder blades.

He went falling to the floor, the gun flying from his grasp.

Mackenzie cried out from the pain in her back as she followed up by driving her knee into the center of the man's back. She could practically feel the air rush out of him and she took advantage of this right away.

She grabbed him by both sides of his head, her right hand nothing more than a glove of blood from his whip attack, and raised it several inches from the ground. Then, with a scream that was a sublime mixture of pain, frustration, and victory, she slammed his head into the wooden floor.

He groaned and gasped.

She did it again, in a quick machine-like motion. Up, then down.

This time, he made no noise.

She rolled off of his back and leaned against the wall. She slid over to Porter and her heart swelled when she saw that he was moving. There was blood coating the left side of his head and he was holding his ear like a frightened child.

"Porter?"

He didn't respond. He did, however, roll over and look at her.

"White?"

He looked worried, wiping blood away from his face.

"The damned gun went off right by my ear," he said, his voice loud. "I can't hear a thing."

She nodded, arching her back and trying to stretch out the pain. But the pain was there to stay, or so it seemed. She reached over to the killer and placed her hand to his neck. It was hard to tell through her own surging adrenaline and heartbeat, but she was fairly certain there was a pulse there.

Mackenzie lay on the floor next to Porter and slowly pulled her cell phone out of her back pocket. When she scrolled for Nelson's number, she left bloody streaks all over the phone.

As the phone started to ring in her ear, she reached out with her free hand and found Porter's. She gave it a squeeze and despite the sticky blood coating her fingers, Porter squeezed back.

CHAPTER THIRTY FIVE

Three days after the Scarecrow Killer had been taken into custody, Mackenzie returned to the same hospital she had left just two days previous with fourteen stitches in her cheek and five along the top of her right hand. She went to the third floor and entered a room that was being occupied by Porter. Seeing him in a hospital bed broke her heart, especially considering how he had ended up there.

He smiled at her when she came in. There was heavy padding and bandaging along the left side of his head but she was relieved to see that all of the IVs had been removed since she last saw him.

"There she is," Porter said.

She smiled, marveling at how much their relationship had changed.

"How are you, Porter?"

"Well, the good news is that I can hear you, which is something the doctors weren't too sure about two days ago. The bad news is that I can't hear you very well. The worse news is that my right ear is never going to look the same again. It seems the bullet actually tore off part of the top."

"I'm so sorry."

"Well, what was I supposed to do?" Porter asked, a little ill-tempered. "Your FBI buddy calls me and tells me that you're planning on trying to find this guy's lair all alone. I had to help."

She shook her head and squeezed his hand.

"How did you find me, anyway?"

"I may have broken into your house," Porter said with a sly smile. "I saw the map you made, pinpointing the location at the center of the cities. Then when I reached the area, I heard gunshots—I guess that's from when you got the jump on him in the shed. So I just followed the commotion."

"Porter, thank you so much. I would have died—"

He shook his head, his jaw set.

"Hell no," he said. "You would have gotten him somehow."

Mackenzie nodded, touched by the compliment, but wasn't so sure. She could still see the killer's face when she closed her eyes, raising that whip, preparing to kill her. She had awakened the last two nights in a panic attack, sweating, alone in bed, and wondered if she would ever stop seeing it.

She found herself getting lost in reverie, and wasn't sure how much time had passed when Porter spoke again.

"So, how's your back?" he asked, quickly changing the subject, probably sensing what was happening to her.

She smiled, forcing herself to snap out of it, forcing herself to stay upbeat. After all, she'd come here to comfort Porter, and she owed him at least that much.

"I had my final X-ray this morning," she said. "Everything checks out. No spinal injuries, just a bad sprain. I was lucky."

"To look at the stitches in your face and my mangled ear, I'm not so sure *lucky* is the word I would use."

Mackenzie went to the visitor's chair by the head of the bed and looked at him with as much sincerity as she could muster.

"I came by to thank you," she said. "And to say goodbye."

He looked alarmed.

"Goodbye?"

She braced herself.

"Yes. Nelson had to make a hard decision. When things got out that I caught the killer after he had taken me off the case, it got ugly."

"He actually *fired* you?"

"No. He suspended me for six months. And after he did that, I quit."

Porter sat up in bed, grimacing but still managing to sneer at Mackenzie.

"Why the hell would you do that?"

She looked to the floor, unsure how to explain it.

"Because," she said, "I spent too much time trying to prove that I wasn't just some young naïve girl that was looking to out-work a mostly older male police force. Now, if you add to that a renegade who openly disregards the chief's rules, that's just something else for me to live down."

He frowned, silent for a long time.

"What do you plan on doing now?" he asked. "You're too good of a detective to be anything else."

She smiled and said: "I'm considering other opportunities."

He grinned at her for a moment and then chuckled.

"You're going to the FBI, aren't you?"

She was sure she did a poor job of hiding her shock. She returned his smile as he reached out and took her hand. It reminded her of their final coherent moments in the killer's house and she found herself wanting to tell him what she had in mind for her future. She left it quiet, though. Now wasn't the time.

159

He'd hit the nail on the head and it had surprised her. Had he always been so perceptive? Had he been hiding some sort of genuine care for her beneath the snark and impatience all this time?

"You *are*," he said. "And good for you. Let's be honest here— that's where you belong. You were always too good for this place. I know that and *you* damn well better know it. I always rode you so hard because I wanted you to be better. I wanted you to get the hell out. And it looks like I did a fine job."

She had expected a reprimand, and she was so touched and relieved by his warmth and his genuine happiness for her.

For the first time in a very long time, she felt tears of gratitude. She managed to keep them in, though, letting the silence speak for them as their hands remained clasped together in a solemn gesture of a friendship that had developed far too late.

CHAPTER THIRTY SIX

It hadn't taken her long to pack. She managed to fit about half of her clothes into two suitcases and put the other half in a cardboard box which she labelled PLEASE DONATE using a Sharpie. Another box contained assorted items such as several paperback books, an old iPad, and a record player she'd once wanted to repair but never got around to. It was labelled the same way.

She had called Zack, fully aware that he was at work and would not be able to take her call. She left him a message that she now regretted as she wheeled her suitcases to the front door. It had been brief and even now, as she looked around at the house, unnaturally empty and cleaned, she wondered if she'd owed him more of an explanation.

That was ridiculous, though. If she owed anyone an explanation, it was herself, for staying stuck in this lifestyle as long as she'd had.

"I'm heading out of town for good," she'd said. "The house is paid for up until the end of next month. It's yours if you want it. If not, the lease will expire and become available. All of your stuff is still here, so come get it whenever you want. You can have the furniture, TV, and anything else we went halves on. I'm starting a new chapter in my life and it's clear that you aren't in it. Please respect my wishes and don't bother calling. Take care, Zack."

The bit about a new chapter was clichéd, but true. It was why she could so easily leave behind thousands of dollar worth of furniture and appliances. It simply wasn't worth the arguments she'd have with Zack over them. It was also why she was leaving half of her clothes. She could buy new clothes—clothes that she'd always wanted to wear but had hesitated to because of what Zack might think, or how Porter or Nelson might react.

This new life she was walking towards offered a new vision of herself that she had only dared to dream of before now. What was the alternative? Was she supposed to stay here and suck up her suspension, then return to work with one more mark against her in a sea of aging men that saw her as an empty threat?

No thanks.

The house had never been so quiet. It was nearly as serene and still as murder scenes she'd seen—almost as stoic as that first cornfield where they'd discovered the first victim. Anything of hers that remained in this house was dead. She felt that with certainty as she reached for the doorknob.

When Mackenzie opened the door and stepped outside, she felt an unseen weight dissolve from her. It only increased as she rolled her suitcases across the small yard and to her car. She put the suitcases in the trunk, slammed it closed, and got behind the wheel.

When she backed out towards the street, she didn't give the house a second look. Her future was in the other direction. All the house represented was a past that she could already feel sliding from her shoulders, a burden she had carried for far longer than she should have.

*

The papers had finally gotten tired of the story. Mackenzie had read it five different ways and no matter how it was told, she still felt as if she were reading about someone else. She had not granted interviews, allowing lazy reporters to assume things. She'd even gone online to the *Oblong Journal* to see if Ellis Pope had written anything about it.

He did not disappoint. He told a story about a violent young woman who thought she was the Punisher, going against her chief's wishes and nabbing the bad guy anyway. While the article had been scathing and hateful, the comments section tore Pope down, heralding Mackenzie as a bad-ass and, according to a few posters, a hottie.

She was reading that particular story on her iPad in the airport when her flight was announced. She grabbed her bags and thought about the call she'd had earlier in the morning with Ellington. It still felt like she had dreamed it all, even as she started towards the gate.

"I wanted to call to let you know that they've asked me to be a part of your initial meeting," he'd said. "Is that going to be okay with you?"

"Yes, that's fine."

"You excited?"

"I am. But I'm nervous more than anything else."

"No need to be. Everyone here is psyched that you're coming. And now it's more than just my praises. The news has been exceptionally kind to you lately. And the fact that you've been humble about it—that speaks volumes."

"Thanks again, by the way," Mackenzie said.

He'd chuckled then and said: "Special Agent White. That sound good to you yet?"

She began to board the ramp to her flight, and stopped to look back at the airport one last time. She expected to take it all in, one last look at her home—but instead, to her horror, she saw the moment she had slammed the killer's head into the floor again and again. She recalled how savage it had made her feel—how absolutely untamed and unpredictable. It had scared her in the days that had followed, but she also knew that it was a part of her now— a part she'd known existed ever since she'd found her father's body.

Now that she had let that part of her out and accepted it as her own, how would that alter the way she worked from now on?

She supposed there was no better way to tell than with a new job where no one knew her. While she wasn't naïve enough to think that it could be a true fresh start, she did, for the first time, believe that she was capable.

She shook away the image and walked down the concourse. A plane was waiting for her.

And so was a new future.

COMING SOON!

Book #2 in the Mackenzie White mystery series!

BOOKS BY BLAKE PIERCE

RILEY PAIGE MYSTERY SERIES
ONCE GONE (Book #1)
ONCE TAKEN (Book #2)
ONCE CRAVED (Book #3)

MACKENZIE WHITE MYSTERY SERIES
BEFORE HE KILLS (Book #1)

Blake Pierce

Blake Pierce is author of the bestselling RILEY PAGE mystery series, which include the mystery suspense thrillers ONCE GONE (book #1), ONCE TAKEN (book #2) and ONCE CRAVED (#3). Blake Pierce is also the author of the MACKENZIE WHITE mystery series.

An avid reader and lifelong fan of the mystery and thriller genres, Blake loves to hear from you, so please feel free to visit www.blakepierceauthor.com to learn more and stay in touch.